this book belongs to
BANBURY CROSSROADS SCHOOL

NICKELODEON

SpongeBob SQUAREPANTS

COMIC CRAZY... Take 2!

DIRECTLY FROM THE PAGES OF NICK magazine

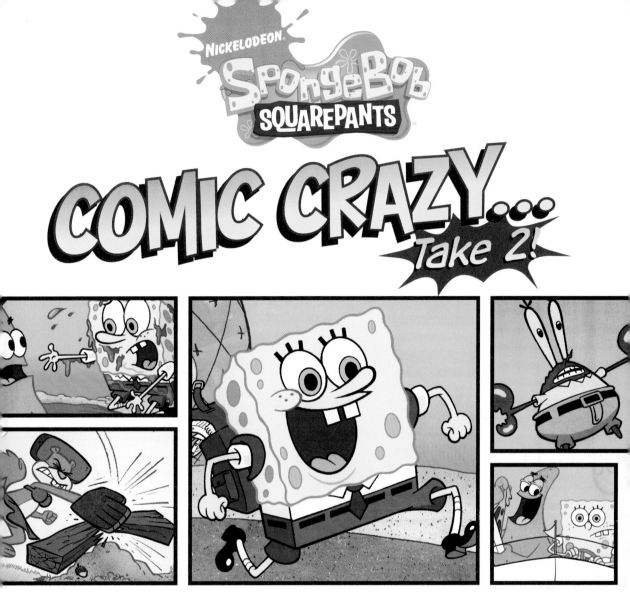

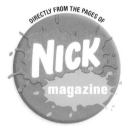

SIMON SPOTLIGHT/NICKELODEON
NEW YORK LONDON TORONTO SYDNEY

SIMON SPOTLIGHT
AN IMPRINT OF SIMON & SCHUSTER CHILDREN'S PUBLISHING DIVISION
1230 AVENUE OF THE AMERICAS, NEW YORK, NEW YORK 10020
© 2010 VIACOM INTERNATIONAL INC. ALL RIGHTS RESERVED. NICKELODEON, *SPONGEBOB SQUAREPANTS*,
AND ALL RELATED TITLES, LOGOS, AND CHARACTERS ARE REGISTERED TRADEMARKS OF VIACOM
INTERNATIONAL INC. CREATED BY STEPHEN HILLENBURG. ALL RIGHTS RESERVED, INCLUDING THE RIGHT OF
REPRODUCTION IN WHOLE OR IN PART IN ANY FORM. SIMON SPOTLIGHT AND COLOPHON ARE REGISTERED
TRADEMARKS OF SIMON & SCHUSTER, INC. FOR INFORMATION ABOUT SPECIAL DISCOUNTS FOR BULK
PURCHASES, PLEASE CONTACT SIMON & SCHUSTER SPECIAL SALES AT 1-866-506-1949 OR
BUSINESS@SIMONANDSCHUSTER.COM. MANUFACTURED IN THE UNITED STATES OF AMERICA 0410 COM
FIRST EDITION
2 4 6 8 10 9 7 5 3 1
ISBN 978-1-4424-0175-4

"TURBO SNAIL," "PSYCHIC SNAIL," AND "SCARY NOISES": STORY, ART, AND LETTERING BY JAMES KOCHALKA. "ACCEPT NO SUBSTITUTES!": STORY BY DAVID LEWMAN; PENCILS BY GREGG SCHIGIEL; INKS BY JEFF ALBRECHT; COLORING BY SNO CONE STUDIOS; LETTERING BY COMICRAFT. "FEARLESS CHEEKS": STORY BY SAM HENDERSON; PENCILS AND INKS BY VINCE DEPORTER; COLORING BY STU CHAIFETZ. "KEEP AWAY FROM KRABS!": STORY, ART, AND INKS BY DAVID LEWMAN; PENCILS BY GREGG SCHIGIEL; INKS BY JEFF ALBRECHT; COLORING BY SNO CONE STUDIOS; LETTERING BY COMICRAFT. "MERMAID MAN CLEANS UP": STORY BY DEREK DRYMON; PENCILS AND INKS BY RAMONA FRADON; COLORING BY MATT MADDEN; LETTERING BY KEN LOPEZ. "THE BIG RACE": STORY, ART, AND LETTERING BY GRAHAM ANNABLE; COLORING BY WES DZIOBA. "DANCE CONTEST": STORY AND ART BY STEPHEN DESTEFANO; COLORING BY WES SHERM COHEN; COLORING BY NICK JENNINGS. "STARING CONTEST": STORY BY JAY LENDER; PENCILS BY GREGG SCHIGIEL; INKS BY JEFF ALBRECHT; DZIOBA; LETTERING BY COMICRAFT. "FINGERS!": STORY AND ART BY STEPHEN DESTEFANO; COLORING BY WES PENCILS AND INKS BY CARL GREENBLATT (SPONGEBOB, ET AL.) AND TED COULDRON (ROBOT AND TREE); PHOTO PANELS BY NICK JENNINGS; LETTERING BY CARL GREENBLATT; COLORING BY DIGITAL CHAMELEON; SPRUCEY THE FIGHTING TREE CREATED BY ANNA S.; TAFU THE ROBOT CREATED BY MAT P. "SPONGEBOB GOES CASUAL": STORY BY JAY LENDER; PENCILS BY GREGG SCHIGIEL; INKS BY JEFF ALBRECHT; COLORING BY SNO CONE STUDIOS; LETTERING BY COMICRAFT. "HAIR TONIC": STORY BY PAUL TIBBITT; PENCILS BY DEREK AND INKS BY ERIK WIESE; COLORING BY NICK JENNINGS; LETTERING BY SHERM COHEN. "HUNGRY FOR HEROES": STORY BY DEREK DRYMON; SPONGEBOB ART BY SHERM COHEN; MERMAID MAN ART BY RAMONA FRADON; COLORING BY SNO CONE STUDIOS; MERMAID MAN LETTERING BY RICK PARKER. "MOLT JOLT": STORY AND LAYOUTS BY JAY LENDER; PENCILS BY GREGG SCHIGIEL; INKS BY JEFF ALBRECHT. COLORING BY SNO CONE STUDIOS; LETTERING BY COMICRAFT. "PATRICK'S PINEAPPLE MAKEOVER": STORY, ART, AND LETTERING BY JAY LENDER; COLORING BY SNO CONE STUDIOS. "SANDY GOES ON A TEAR": STORY BY SAM HENDERSON; PENCILS AND INKS BY VINCE DEPORTER; COLORING BY STU CHAIFETZ; EDITED BY DAVE ROMAN.

NICK MAGAZINE SPONGEBOB COMIC STAFF: ANDREW BRISMAN, CHRIS DUFFY, LAURA GALEN, TIM JONES, FRANK PITTARESE, DAVID ROMAN, TINA STRASBERG, CATHERINE TUTRONE, AND PAUL TUTRONE. NICK MAG WOULD LIKE TO THANK STEPHEN HILLENBURG, DEREK DRYMON, AND SHERM COHEN.

SPECIAL THANKS TO STU CHAIFETZ.

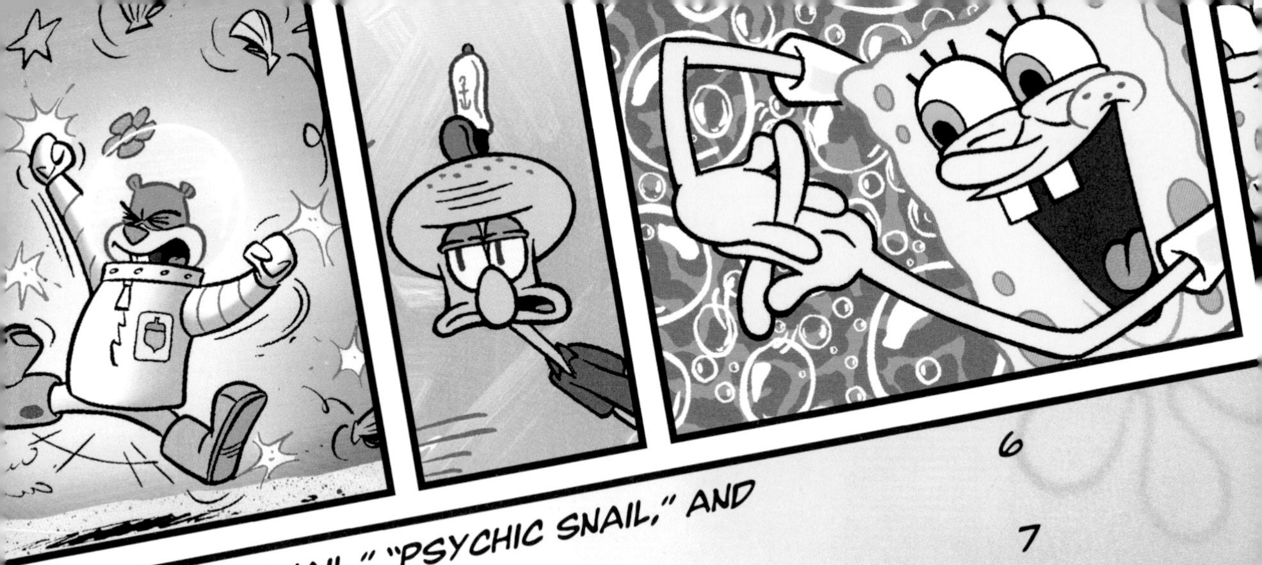

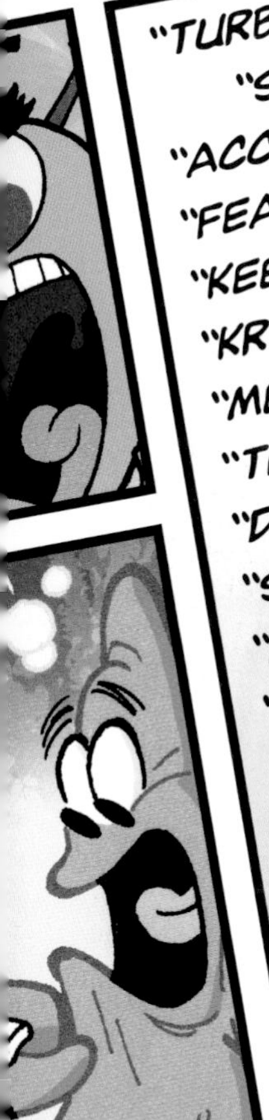

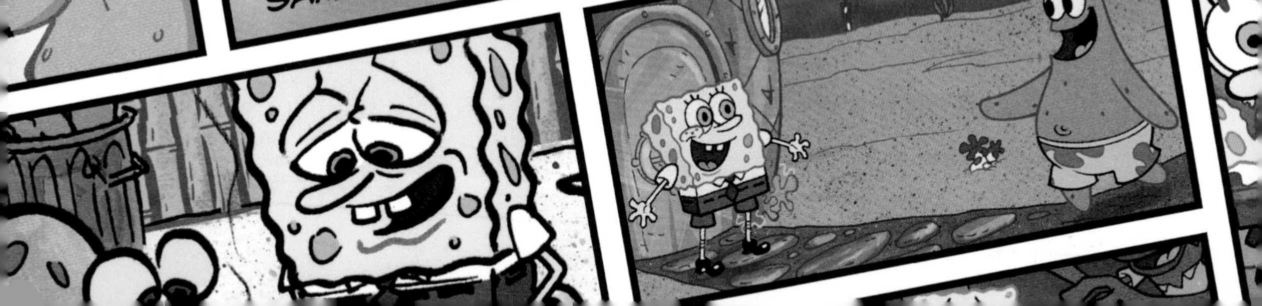

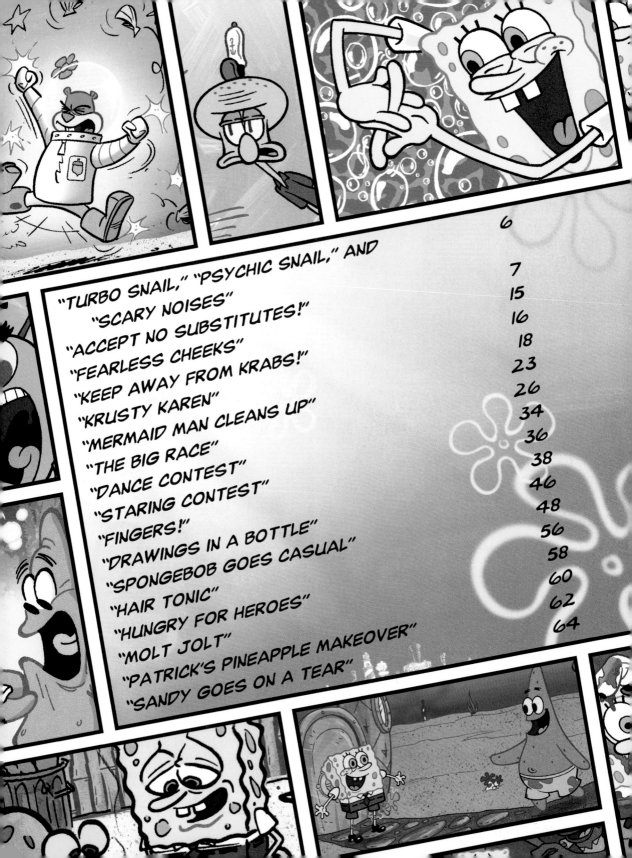

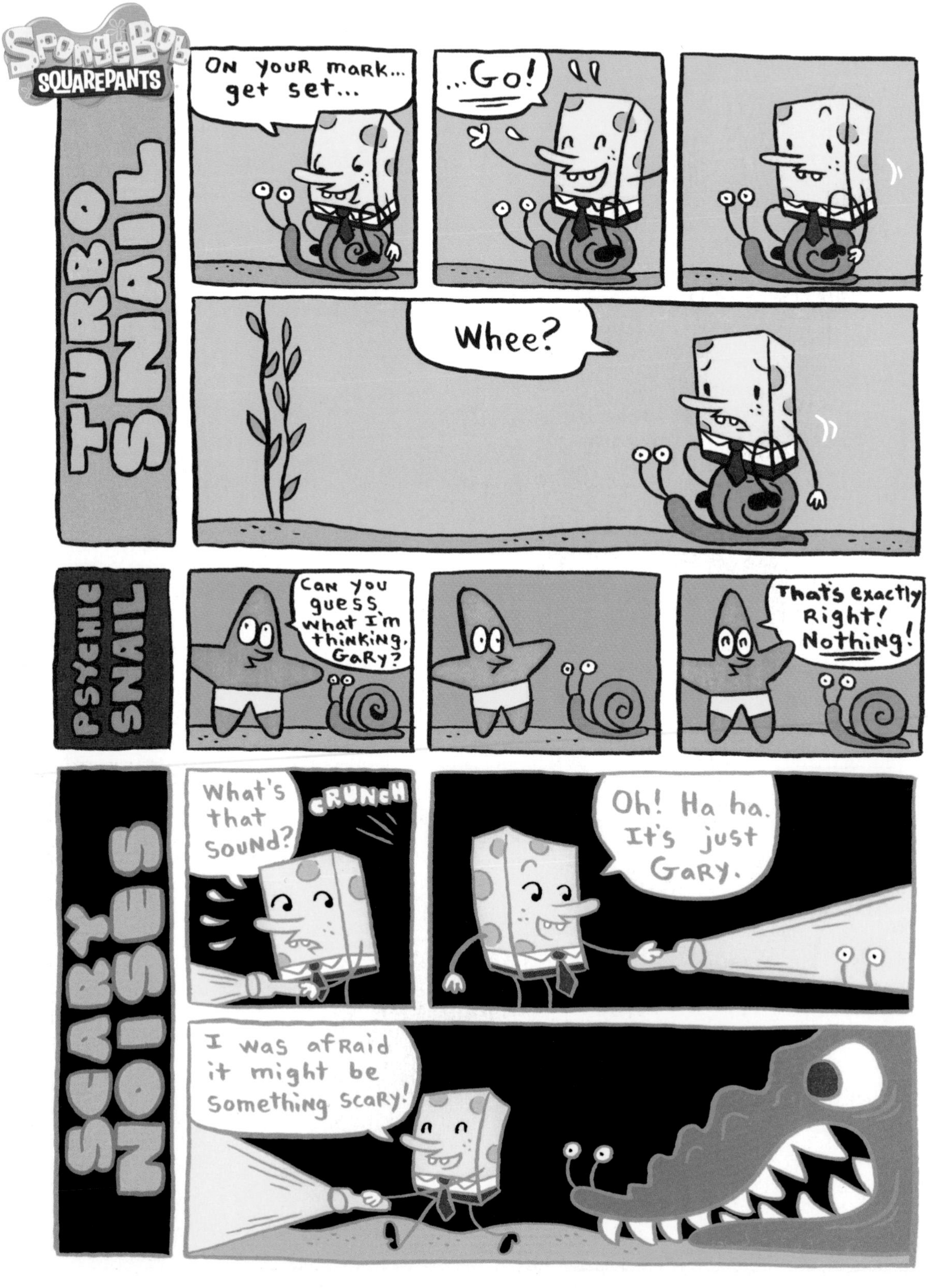
SpongeBob SquarePants
TURBO SNAIL
ON YOUR mark... get set...
...Go!
Whee?
PSYCHIC SNAIL
Can you guess what I'm thinking, Gary?
That's exactly Right! Nothing!
SCARY NOISES
What's that sound?
CRUNCH
Oh! Ha ha. It's just Gary.
I was afraid it might be something scary!

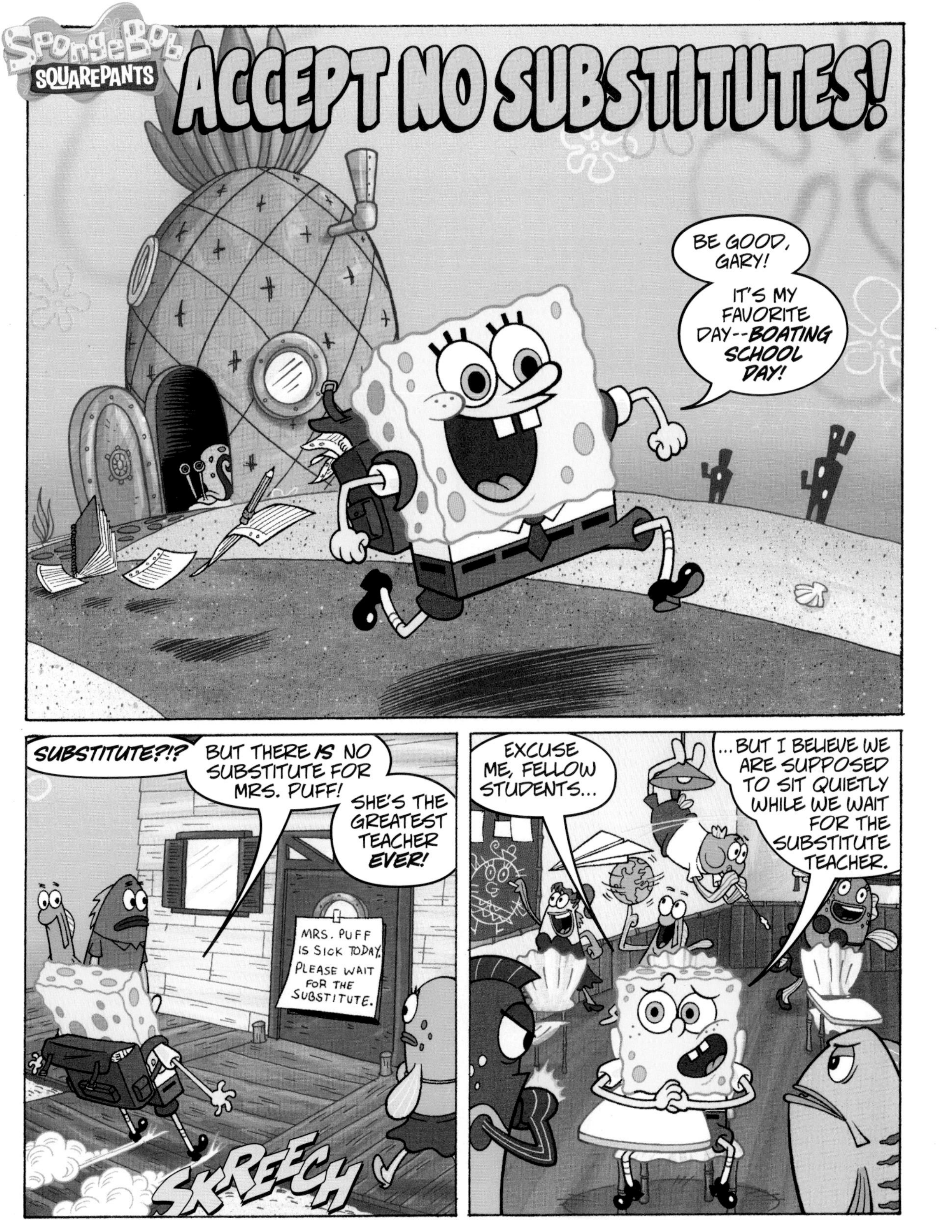
SpongeBob SQUAREPANTS
ACCEPT NO SUBSTITUTES!
BE GOOD, GARY!
IT'S MY FAVORITE DAY--BOATING SCHOOL DAY!
SUBSTITUTE?!?
BUT THERE IS NO SUBSTITUTE FOR MRS. PUFF!
SHE'S THE GREATEST TEACHER EVER!
MRS. PUFF IS SICK TODAY. PLEASE WAIT FOR THE SUBSTITUTE.
SKREECH
EXCUSE ME, FELLOW STUDENTS...
...BUT I BELIEVE WE ARE SUPPOSED TO SIT QUIETLY WHILE WE WAIT FOR THE SUBSTITUTE TEACHER.

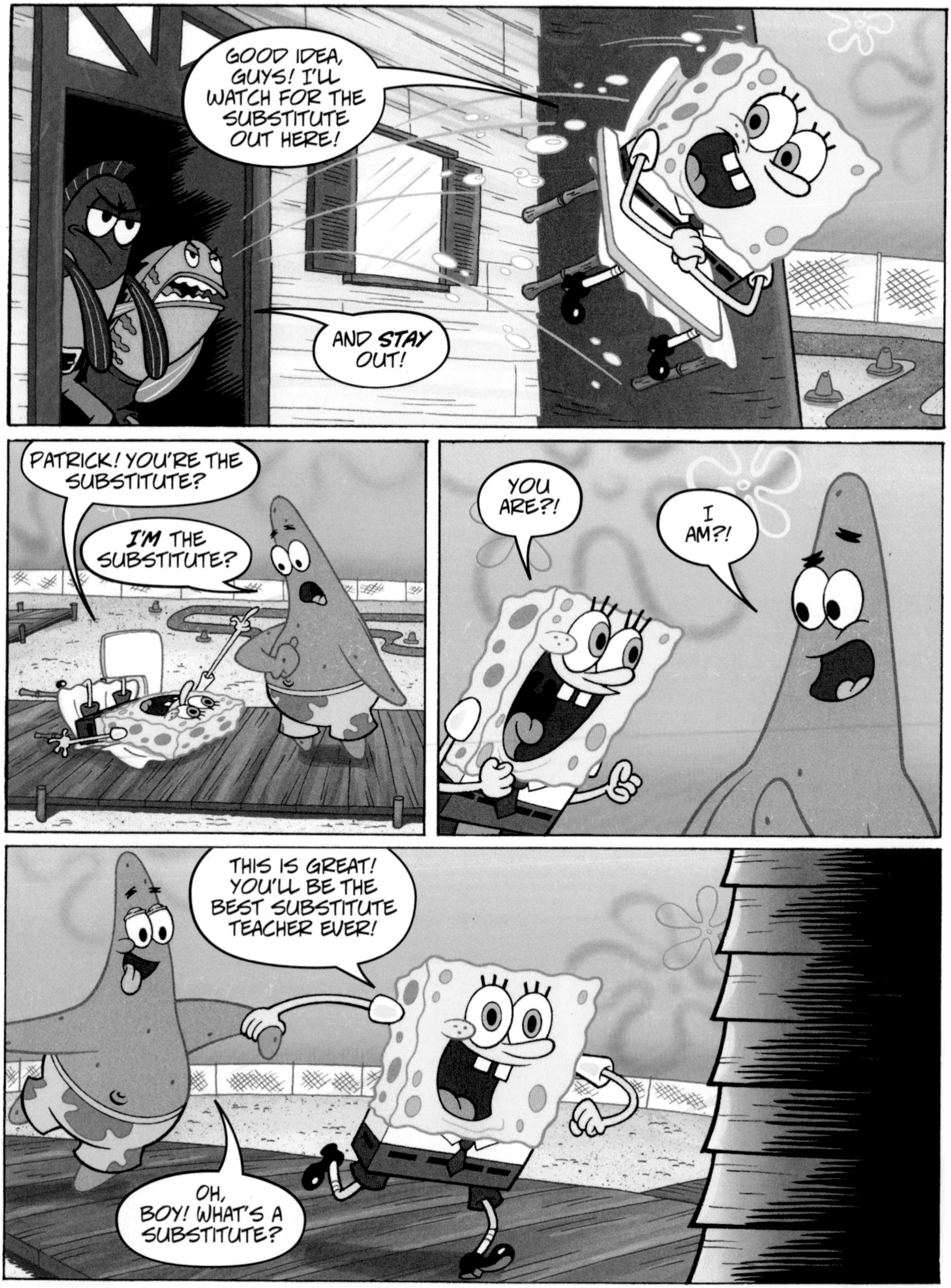
GOOD IDEA, GUYS! I'LL WATCH FOR THE SUBSTITUTE OUT HERE!
AND **STAY** OUT!
PATRICK! YOU'RE THE SUBSTITUTE?
I'M THE SUBSTITUTE?
YOU ARE?!
I AM?!
THIS IS GREAT! YOU'LL BE THE BEST SUBSTITUTE TEACHER EVER!
OH, BOY! WHAT'S A SUBSTITUTE?

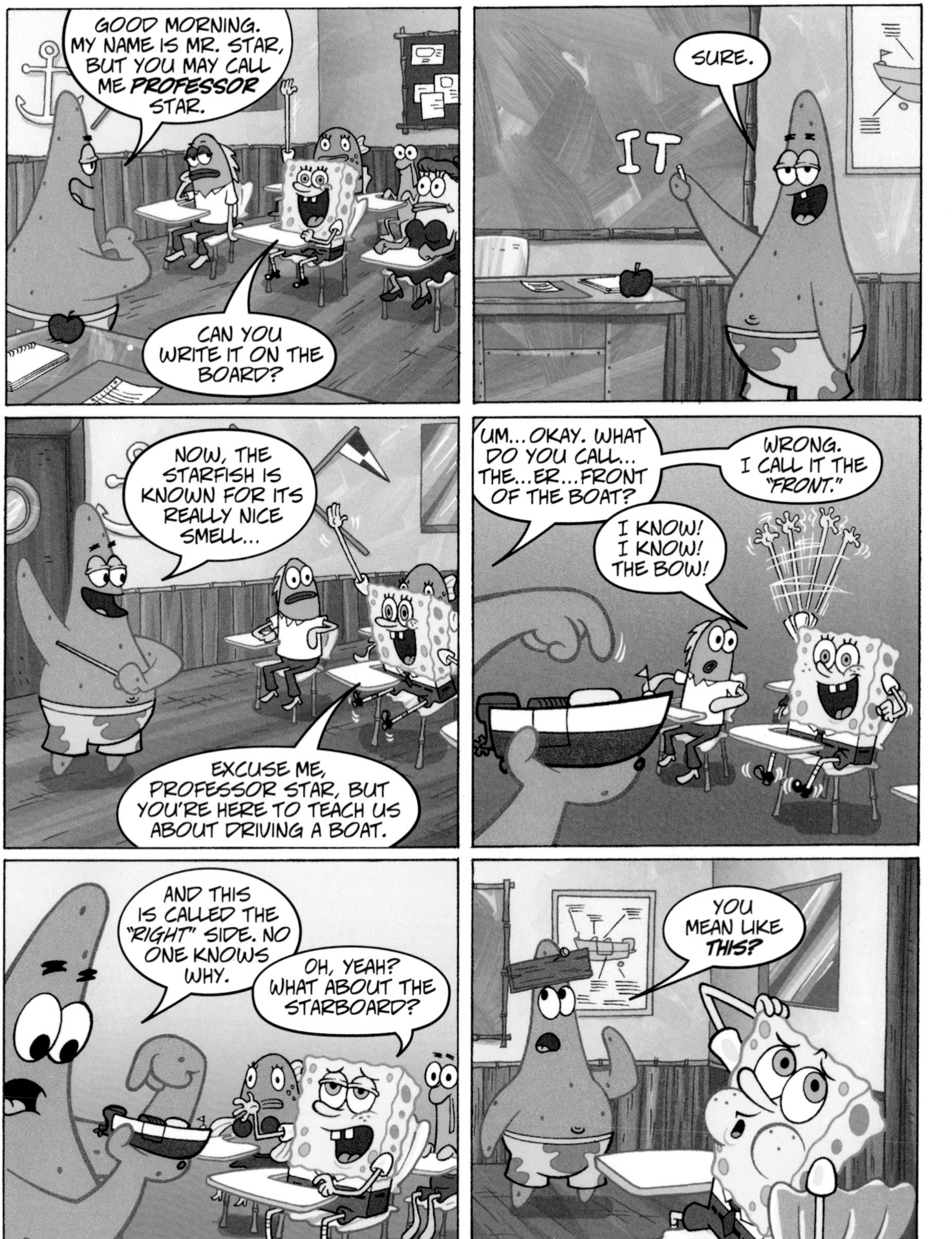
GOOD MORNING. MY NAME IS MR. STAR, BUT YOU MAY CALL ME **PROFESSOR** STAR.
CAN YOU WRITE IT ON THE BOARD?
SURE.
IT
NOW, THE STARFISH IS KNOWN FOR ITS REALLY NICE SMELL...
EXCUSE ME, PROFESSOR STAR, BUT YOU'RE HERE TO TEACH US ABOUT DRIVING A BOAT.
UM...OKAY. WHAT DO YOU CALL... THE...ER...FRONT OF THE BOAT?
I KNOW! I KNOW! THE BOW!
WRONG. I CALL IT THE *"FRONT."*
AND THIS IS CALLED THE *"RIGHT"* SIDE. NO ONE KNOWS WHY.
OH, YEAH? WHAT ABOUT THE STARBOARD?
YOU MEAN LIKE ***THIS?***

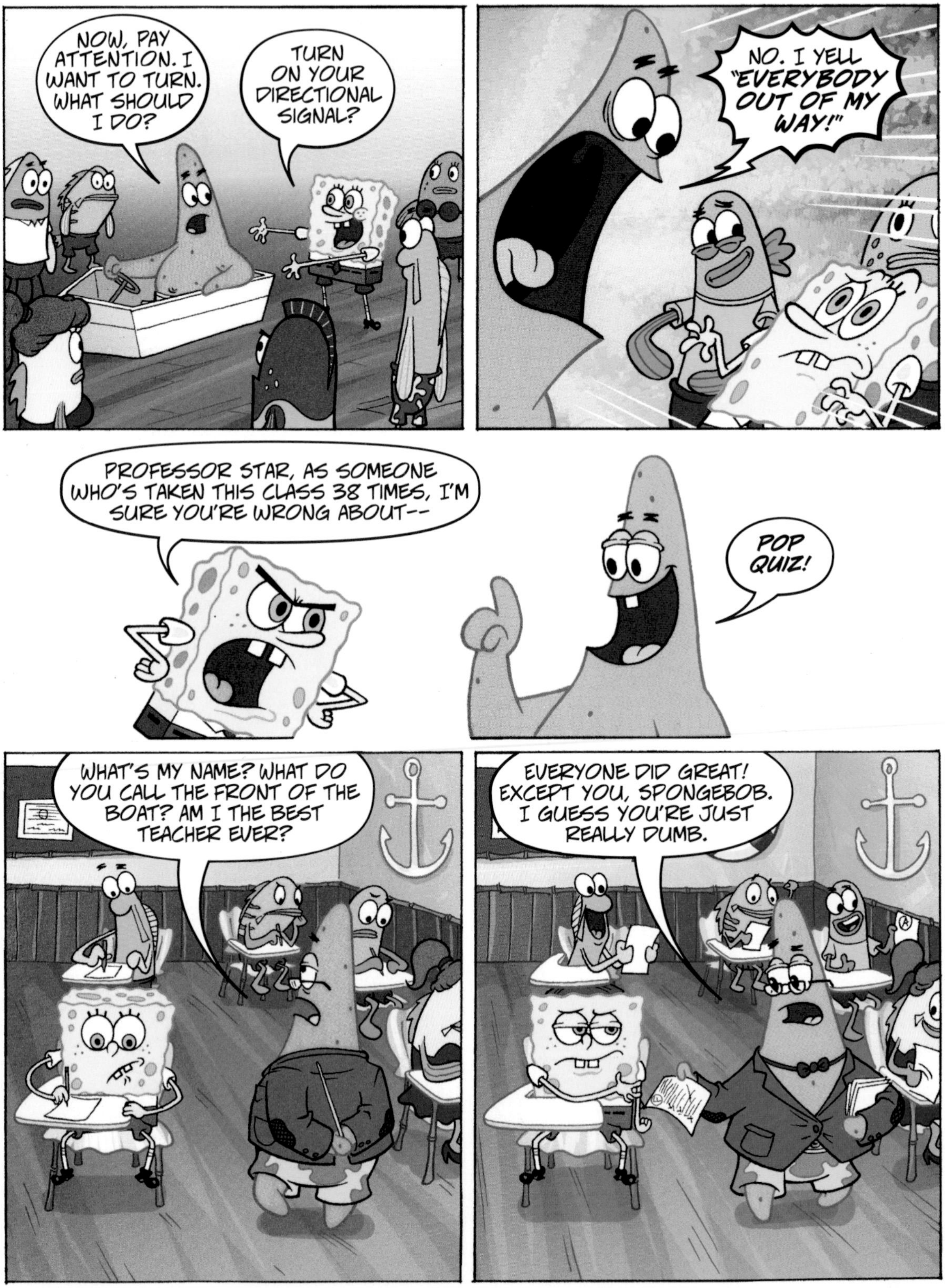
NOW, PAY ATTENTION. I WANT TO TURN. WHAT SHOULD I DO?
TURN ON YOUR DIRECTIONAL SIGNAL?
NO. I YELL "EVERYBODY OUT OF MY WAY!"
PROFESSOR STAR, AS SOMEONE WHO'S TAKEN THIS CLASS 38 TIMES, I'M SURE YOU'RE WRONG ABOUT--
POP QUIZ!
WHAT'S MY NAME? WHAT DO YOU CALL THE FRONT OF THE BOAT? AM I THE BEST TEACHER EVER?
EVERYONE DID GREAT! EXCEPT YOU, SPONGEBOB. I GUESS YOU'RE JUST REALLY DUMB.

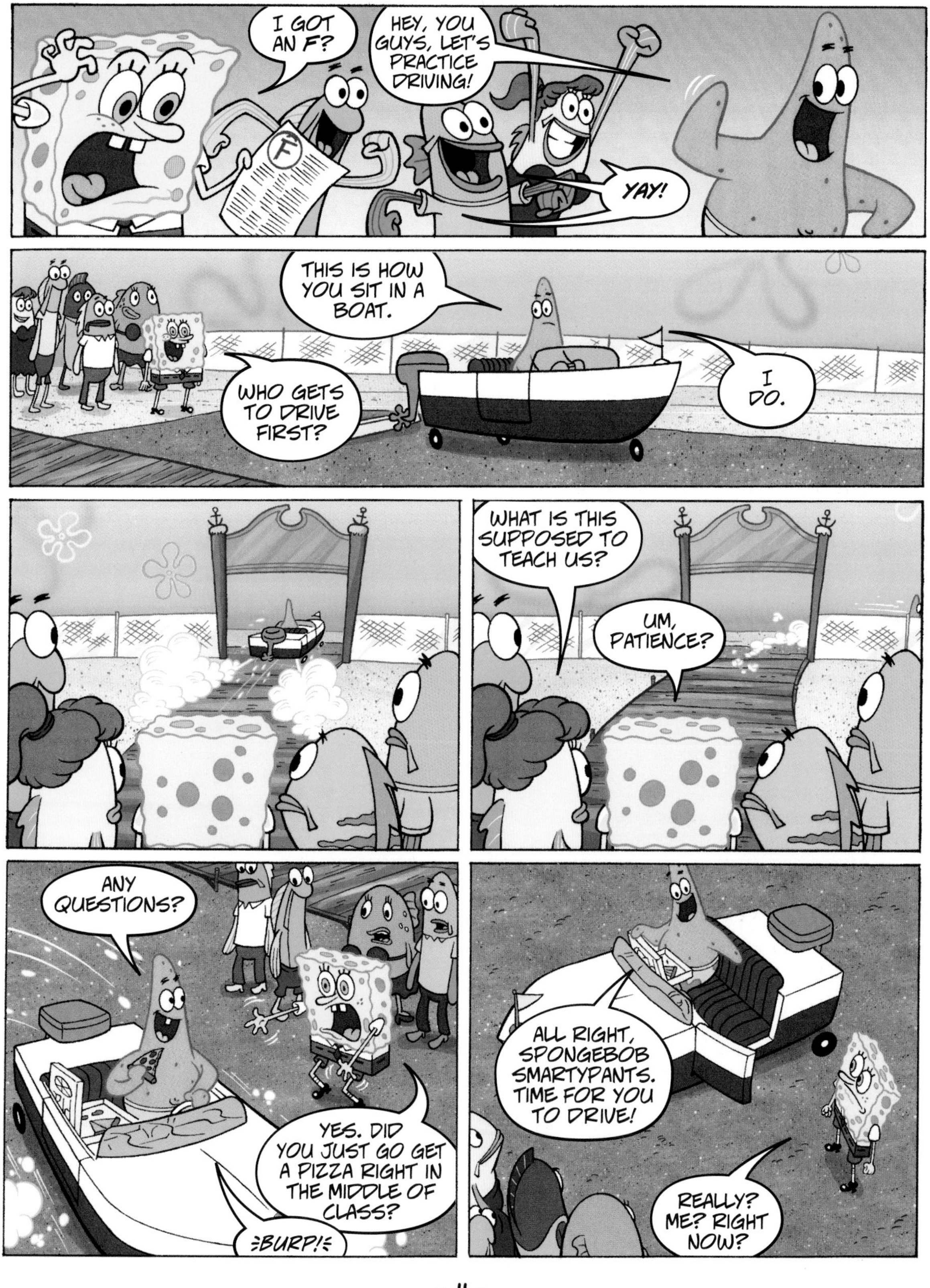
I GOT AN F?
HEY, YOU GUYS, LET'S PRACTICE DRIVING!
YAY!
THIS IS HOW YOU SIT IN A BOAT.
WHO GETS TO DRIVE FIRST?
I DO.
WHAT IS THIS SUPPOSED TO TEACH US?
UM, PATIENCE?
ANY QUESTIONS?
YES. DID YOU JUST GO GET A PIZZA RIGHT IN THE MIDDLE OF CLASS?
BURP!
ALL RIGHT, SPONGEBOB SMARTYPANTS. TIME FOR YOU TO DRIVE!
REALLY? ME? RIGHT NOW?

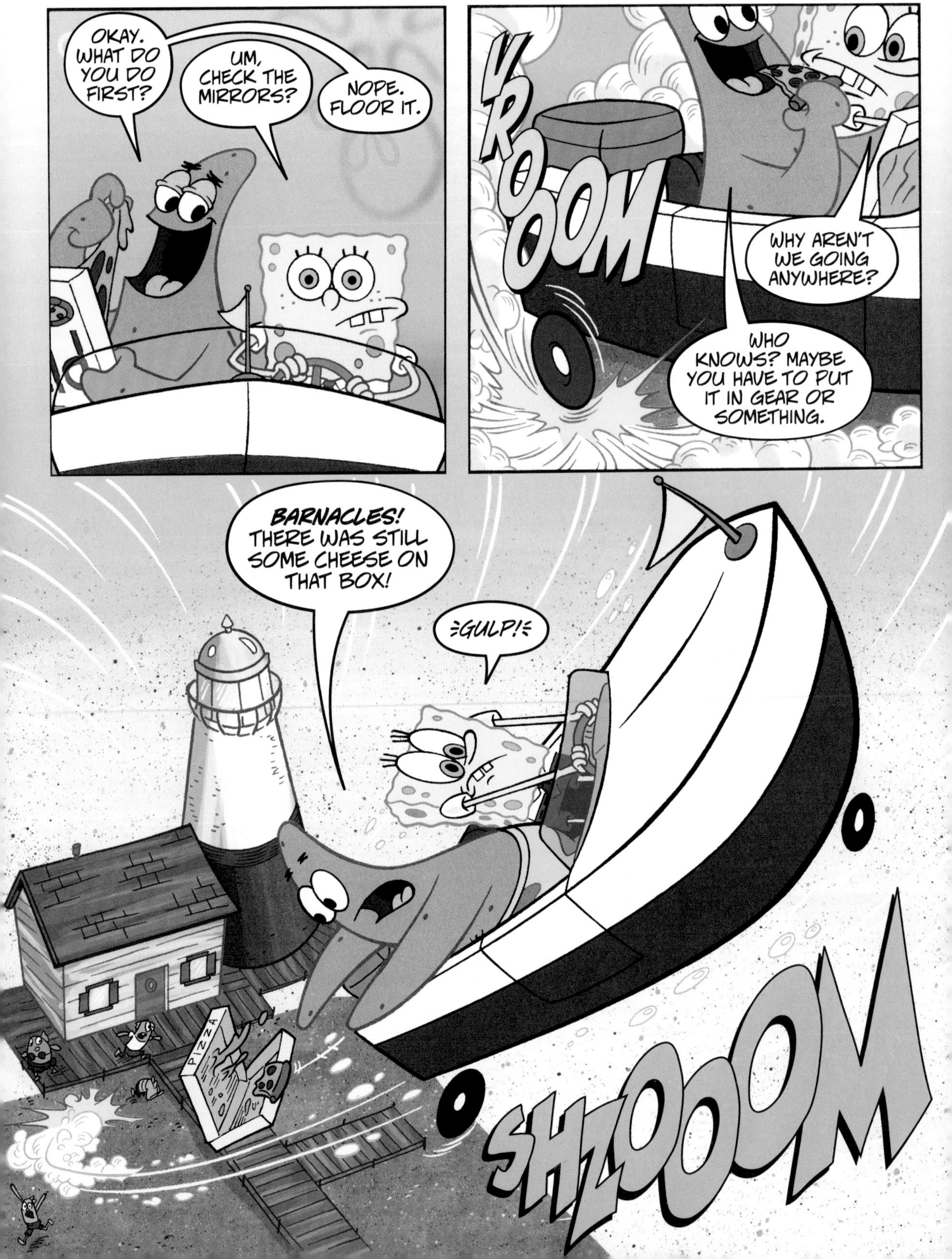
OKAY. WHAT DO YOU DO FIRST?
UM, CHECK THE MIRRORS?
NOPE. FLOOR IT.
VROOOM
WHY AREN'T WE GOING ANYWHERE?
WHO KNOWS? MAYBE YOU HAVE TO PUT IT IN GEAR OR SOMETHING.
BARNACLES! THERE WAS STILL SOME CHEESE ON THAT BOX!
GULP!
PIZZA
SHZOOOM

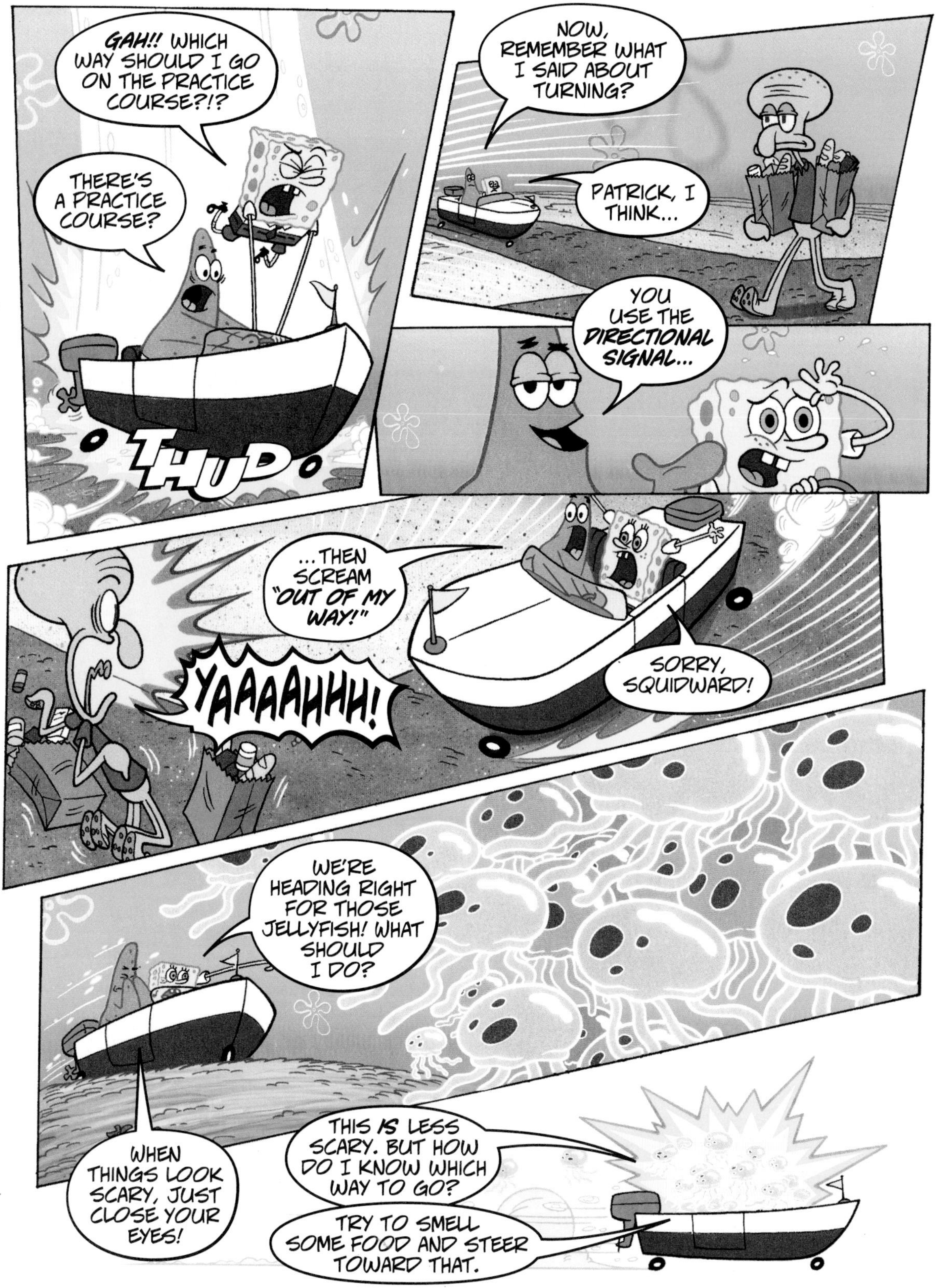
GAH!! WHICH WAY SHOULD I GO ON THE PRACTICE COURSE?!?
THERE'S A PRACTICE COURSE?
THUD
NOW, REMEMBER WHAT I SAID ABOUT TURNING?
PATRICK, I THINK...
YOU USE THE DIRECTIONAL SIGNAL...
...THEN SCREAM "OUT OF MY WAY!"
YAAAAHHH!
SORRY, SQUIDWARD!
WE'RE HEADING RIGHT FOR THOSE JELLYFISH! WHAT SHOULD I DO?
WHEN THINGS LOOK SCARY, JUST CLOSE YOUR EYES!
THIS IS LESS SCARY. BUT HOW DO I KNOW WHICH WAY TO GO?
TRY TO SMELL SOME FOOD AND STEER TOWARD THAT.

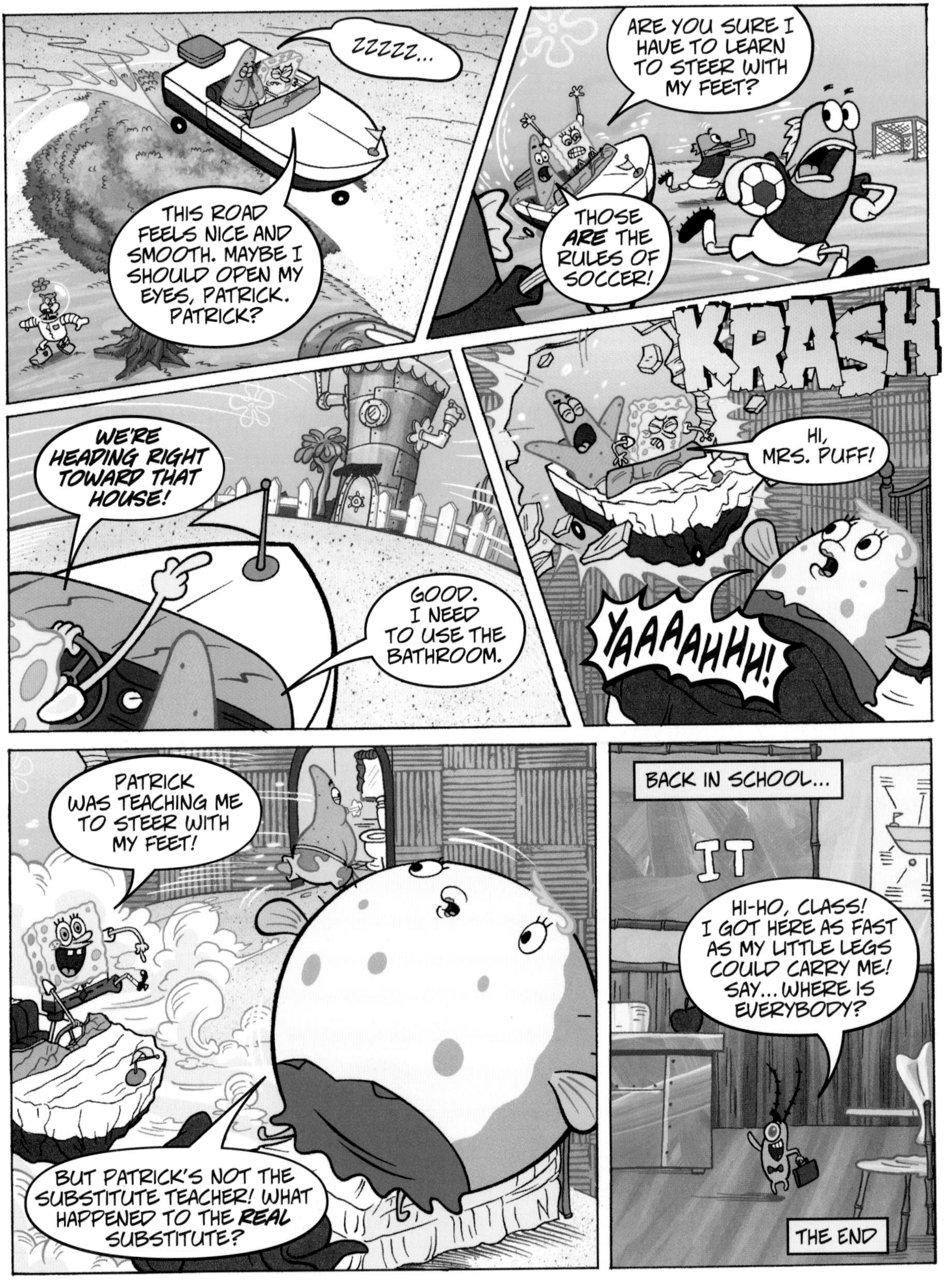
ZZZZZ...
THIS ROAD FEELS NICE AND SMOOTH. MAYBE I SHOULD OPEN MY EYES, PATRICK. PATRICK?
ARE YOU SURE I HAVE TO LEARN TO STEER WITH MY FEET?
THOSE ARE THE RULES OF SOCCER!
WE'RE HEADING RIGHT TOWARD THAT HOUSE!
GOOD. I NEED TO USE THE BATHROOM.
KRASH
HI, MRS. PUFF!
YAAAAHHH!
PATRICK WAS TEACHING ME TO STEER WITH MY FEET!
BUT PATRICK'S NOT THE SUBSTITUTE TEACHER! WHAT HAPPENED TO THE REAL SUBSTITUTE?
BACK IN SCHOOL...
IT
HI-HO, CLASS! I GOT HERE AS FAST AS MY LITTLE LEGS COULD CARRY ME! SAY... WHERE IS EVERYBODY?
THE END

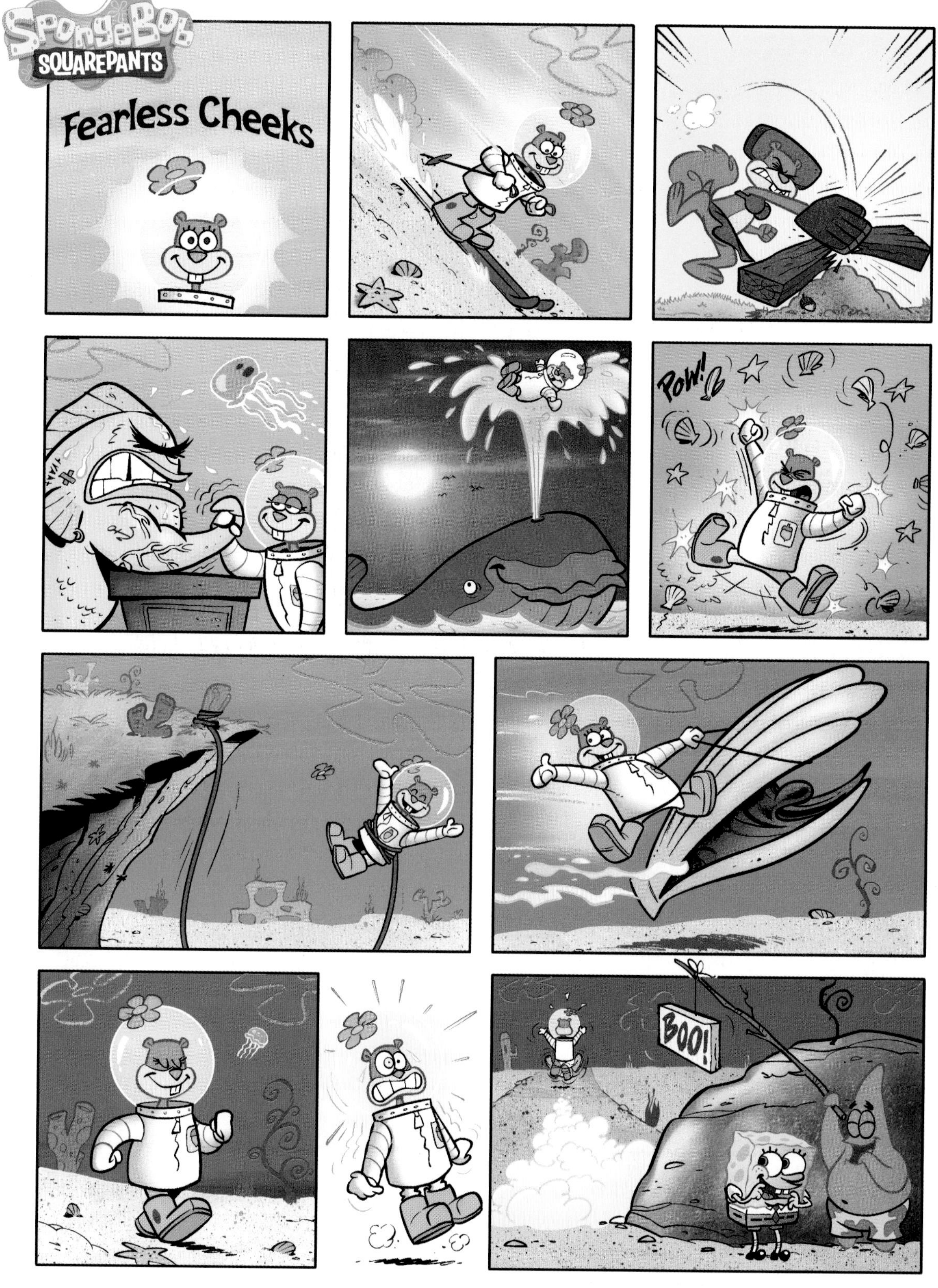
SpongeBob SquarePants
Fearless Cheeks
POW!
BOO!

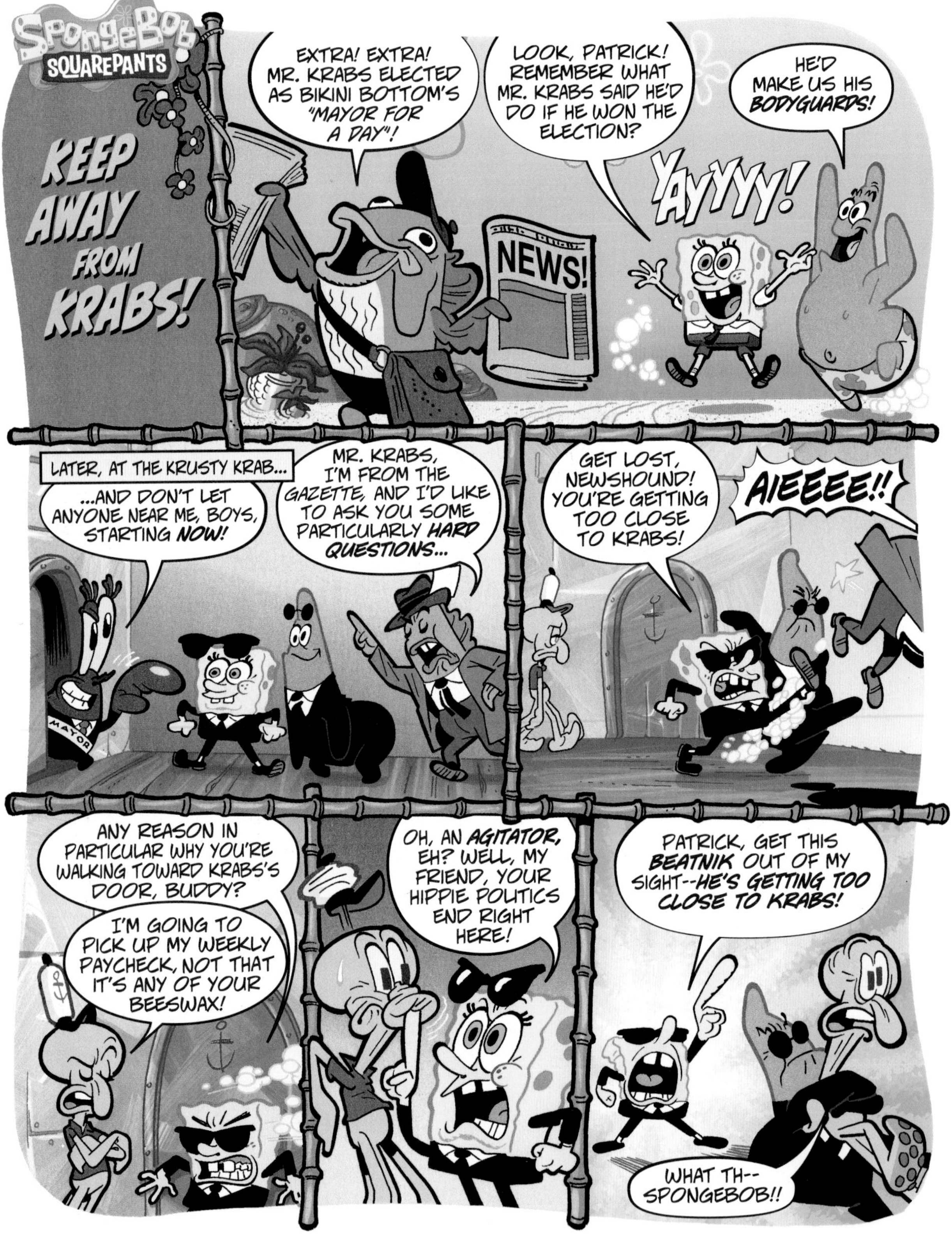
SpongeBob SQUAREPANTS
KEEP AWAY FROM KRABS!
EXTRA! EXTRA! MR. KRABS ELECTED AS BIKINI BOTTOM'S "MAYOR FOR A DAY"!
NEWS!
LOOK, PATRICK! REMEMBER WHAT MR. KRABS SAID HE'D DO IF HE WON THE ELECTION?
HE'D MAKE US HIS BODYGUARDS!
YAYYYY!
LATER, AT THE KRUSTY KRAB...
...AND DON'T LET ANYONE NEAR ME, BOYS, STARTING NOW!
MAYOR
MR. KRABS, I'M FROM THE GAZETTE, AND I'D LIKE TO ASK YOU SOME PARTICULARLY HARD QUESTIONS...
GET LOST, NEWSHOUND! YOU'RE GETTING TOO CLOSE TO KRABS!
AIEEEE!!
ANY REASON IN PARTICULAR WHY YOU'RE WALKING TOWARD KRABS'S DOOR, BUDDY?
I'M GOING TO PICK UP MY WEEKLY PAYCHECK, NOT THAT IT'S ANY OF YOUR BEESWAX!
OH, AN AGITATOR, EH? WELL, MY FRIEND, YOUR HIPPIE POLITICS END RIGHT HERE!
PATRICK, GET THIS BEATNIK OUT OF MY SIGHT--HE'S GETTING TOO CLOSE TO KRABS!
WHAT TH-- SPONGEBOB!!

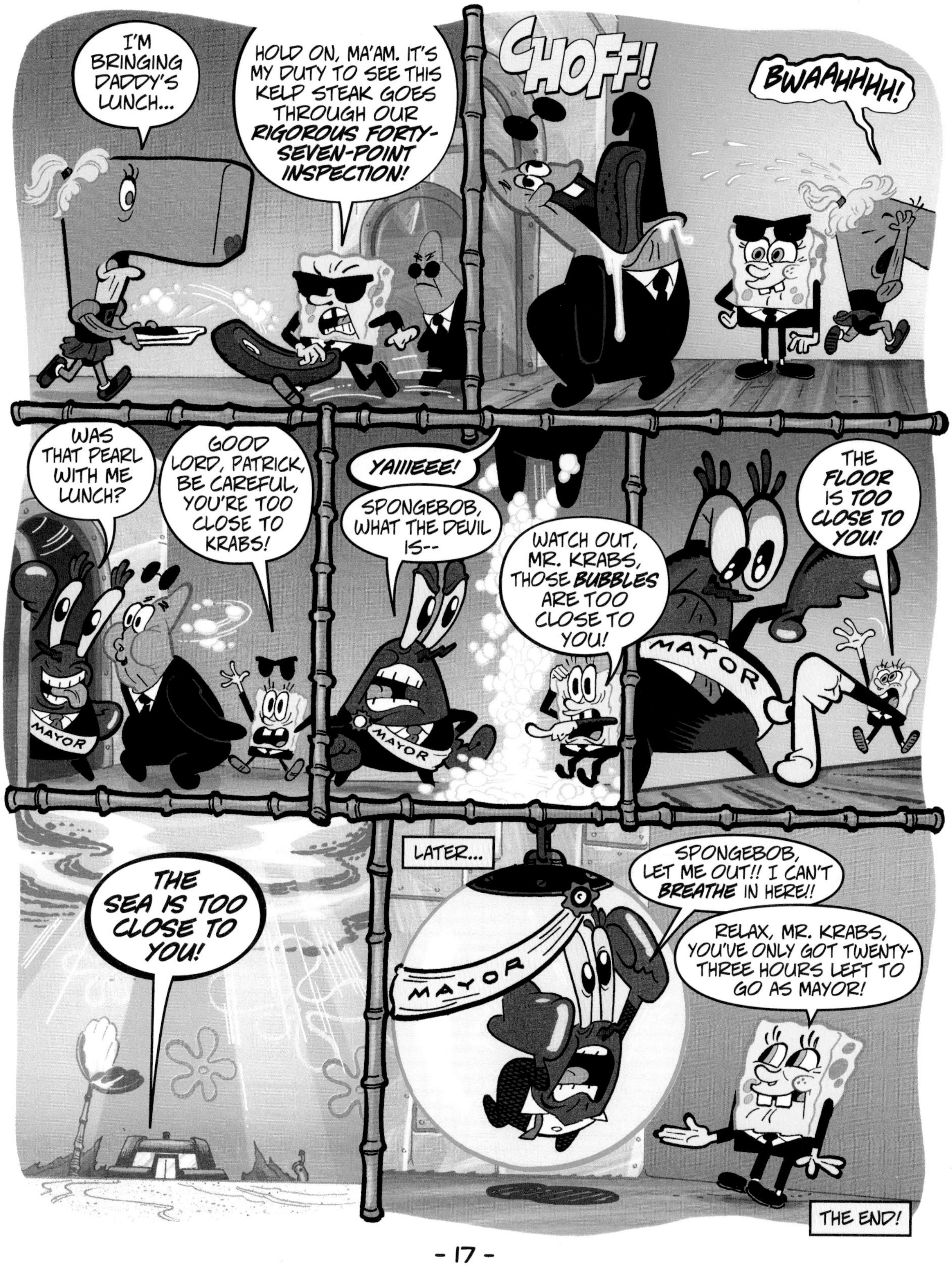
I'M BRINGING DADDY'S LUNCH...
HOLD ON, MA'AM. IT'S MY DUTY TO SEE THIS KELP STEAK GOES THROUGH OUR RIGOROUS FORTY-SEVEN-POINT INSPECTION!
CHOFF!
BWAAHHHH!
WAS THAT PEARL WITH ME LUNCH?
GOOD LORD, PATRICK, BE CAREFUL, YOU'RE TOO CLOSE TO KRABS!
YAIIIEEE!
SPONGEBOB, WHAT THE DEVIL IS--
MAYOR
WATCH OUT, MR. KRABS, THOSE BUBBLES ARE TOO CLOSE TO YOU!
THE FLOOR IS TOO CLOSE TO YOU!
THE SEA IS TOO CLOSE TO YOU!
LATER...
SPONGEBOB, LET ME OUT!! I CAN'T BREATHE IN HERE!!
RELAX, MR. KRABS, YOU'VE ONLY GOT TWENTY-THREE HOURS LEFT TO GO AS MAYOR!
THE END!

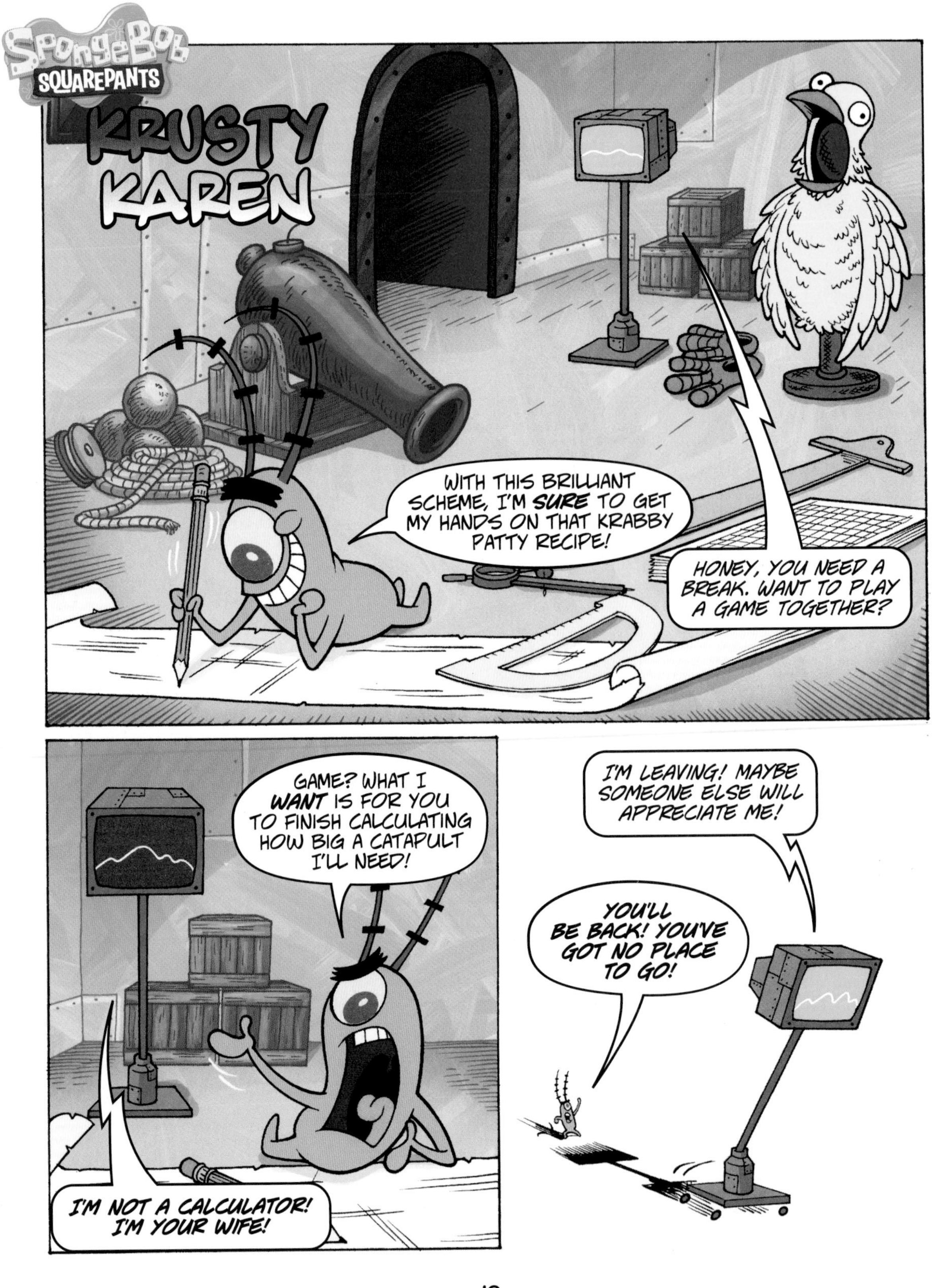
SPONGEBOB SQUAREPANTS
KRUSTY KAREN
WITH THIS BRILLIANT SCHEME, I'M SURE TO GET MY HANDS ON THAT KRABBY PATTY RECIPE!
HONEY, YOU NEED A BREAK. WANT TO PLAY A GAME TOGETHER?
GAME? WHAT I WANT IS FOR YOU TO FINISH CALCULATING HOW BIG A CATAPULT I'LL NEED!
I'M NOT A CALCULATOR! I'M YOUR WIFE!
I'M LEAVING! MAYBE SOMEONE ELSE WILL APPRECIATE ME!
YOU'LL BE BACK! YOU'VE GOT NO PLACE TO GO!

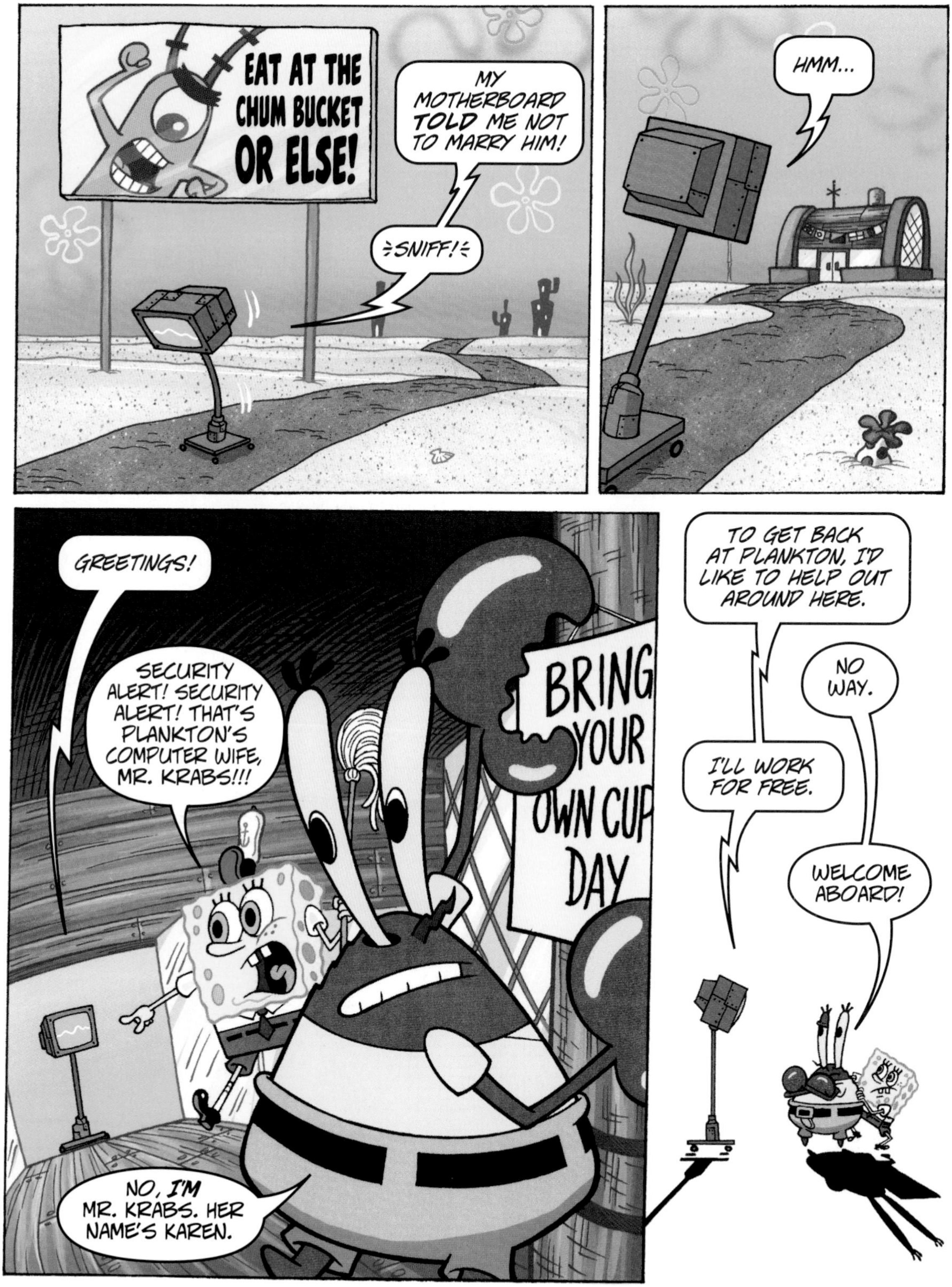
EAT AT THE CHUM BUCKET OR ELSE!
MY MOTHERBOARD TOLD ME NOT TO MARRY HIM!
SNIFF!
HMM...
GREETINGS!
SECURITY ALERT! SECURITY ALERT! THAT'S PLANKTON'S COMPUTER WIFE, MR. KRABS!!!
NO, I'M MR. KRABS. HER NAME'S KAREN.
BRING YOUR OWN CUP DAY
TO GET BACK AT PLANKTON, I'D LIKE TO HELP OUT AROUND HERE.
NO WAY.
I'LL WORK FOR FREE.
WELCOME ABOARD!

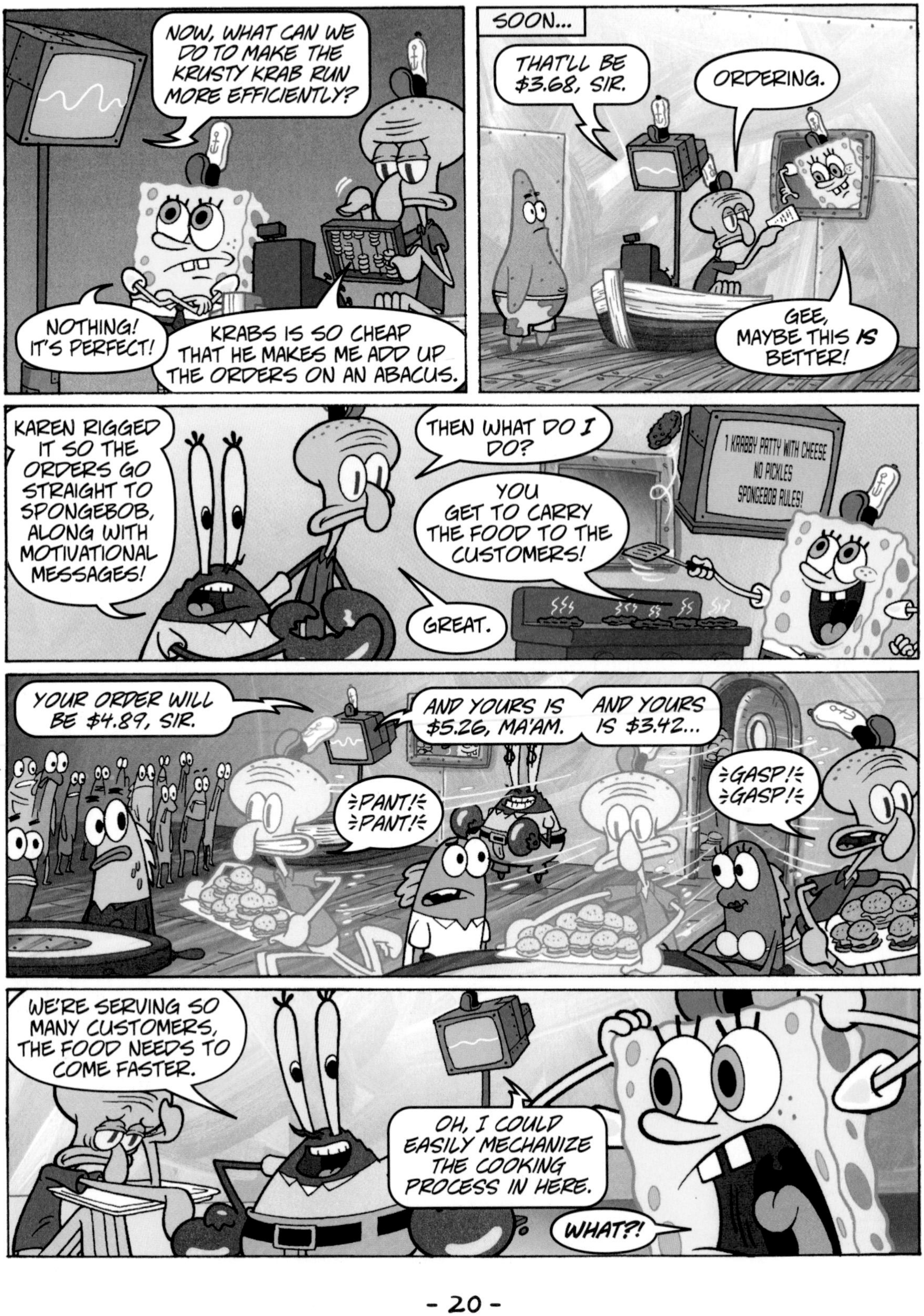
NOW, WHAT CAN WE DO TO MAKE THE KRUSTY KRAB RUN MORE EFFICIENTLY?
NOTHING! IT'S PERFECT!
KRABS IS SO CHEAP THAT HE MAKES ME ADD UP THE ORDERS ON AN ABACUS.
SOON...
THAT'LL BE $3.68, SIR.
ORDERING.
GEE, MAYBE THIS IS BETTER!
KAREN RIGGED IT SO THE ORDERS GO STRAIGHT TO SPONGEBOB, ALONG WITH MOTIVATIONAL MESSAGES!
THEN WHAT DO I DO?
YOU GET TO CARRY THE FOOD TO THE CUSTOMERS!
GREAT.
1 KRABBY PATTY WITH CHEESE
NO PICKLES
SPONGEBOB RULES!
YOUR ORDER WILL BE $4.89, SIR.
AND YOURS IS $5.26, MA'AM.
AND YOURS IS $3.42...
PANT! PANT!
GASP! GASP!
WE'RE SERVING SO MANY CUSTOMERS, THE FOOD NEEDS TO COME FASTER.
OH, I COULD EASILY MECHANIZE THE COOKING PROCESS IN HERE.
WHAT?!

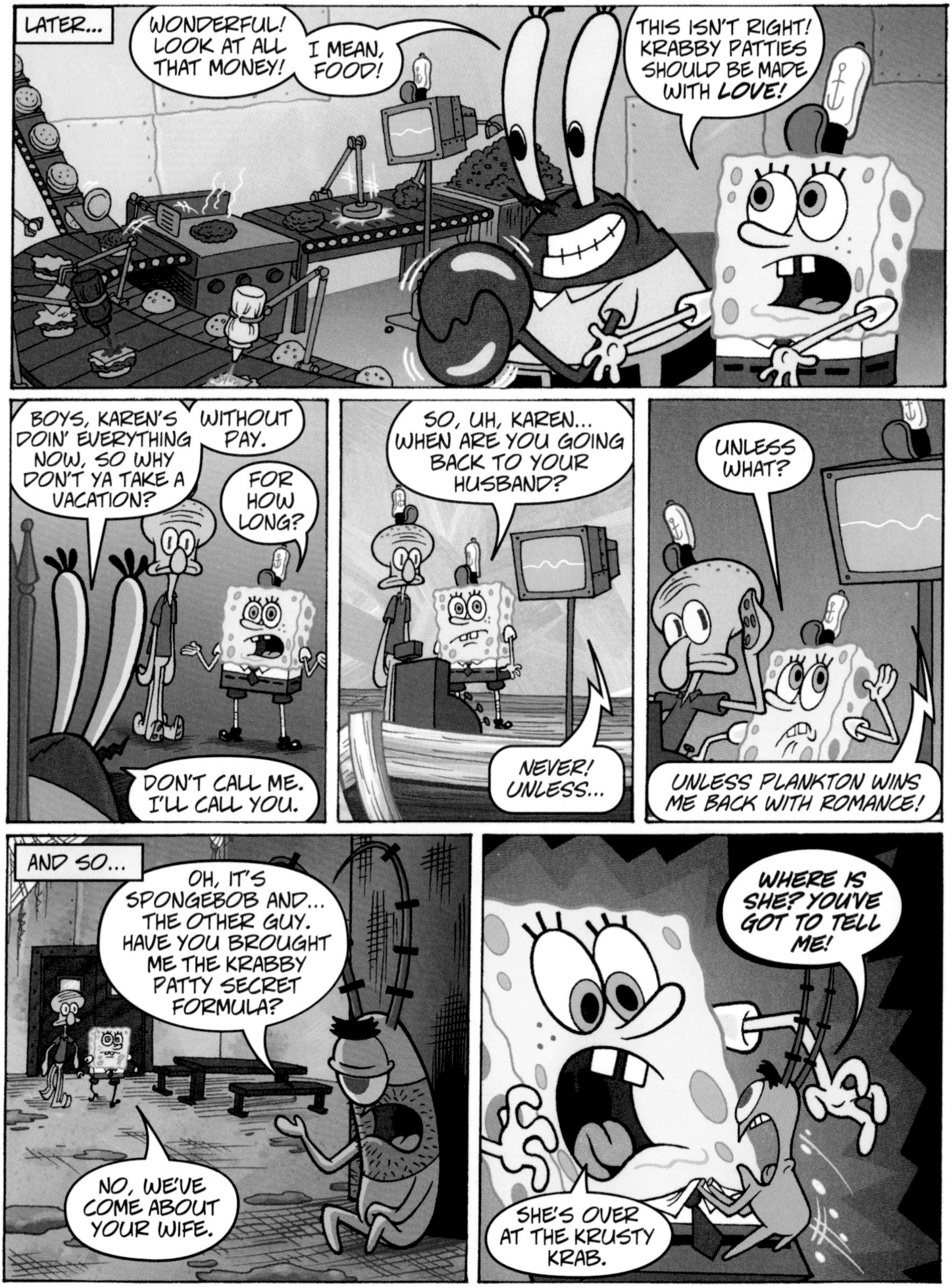
LATER...
WONDERFUL! LOOK AT ALL THAT MONEY!
I MEAN, FOOD!
THIS ISN'T RIGHT! KRABBY PATTIES SHOULD BE MADE WITH LOVE!
BOYS, KAREN'S DOIN' EVERYTHING NOW, SO WHY DON'T YA TAKE A VACATION?
WITHOUT PAY.
FOR HOW LONG?
DON'T CALL ME. I'LL CALL YOU.
SO, UH, KAREN... WHEN ARE YOU GOING BACK TO YOUR HUSBAND?
NEVER! UNLESS...
UNLESS WHAT?
UNLESS PLANKTON WINS ME BACK WITH ROMANCE!
AND SO...
OH, IT'S SPONGEBOB AND... THE OTHER GUY. HAVE YOU BROUGHT ME THE KRABBY PATTY SECRET FORMULA?
NO, WE'VE COME ABOUT YOUR WIFE.
WHERE IS SHE? YOU'VE GOT TO TELL ME!
SHE'S OVER AT THE KRUSTY KRAB.

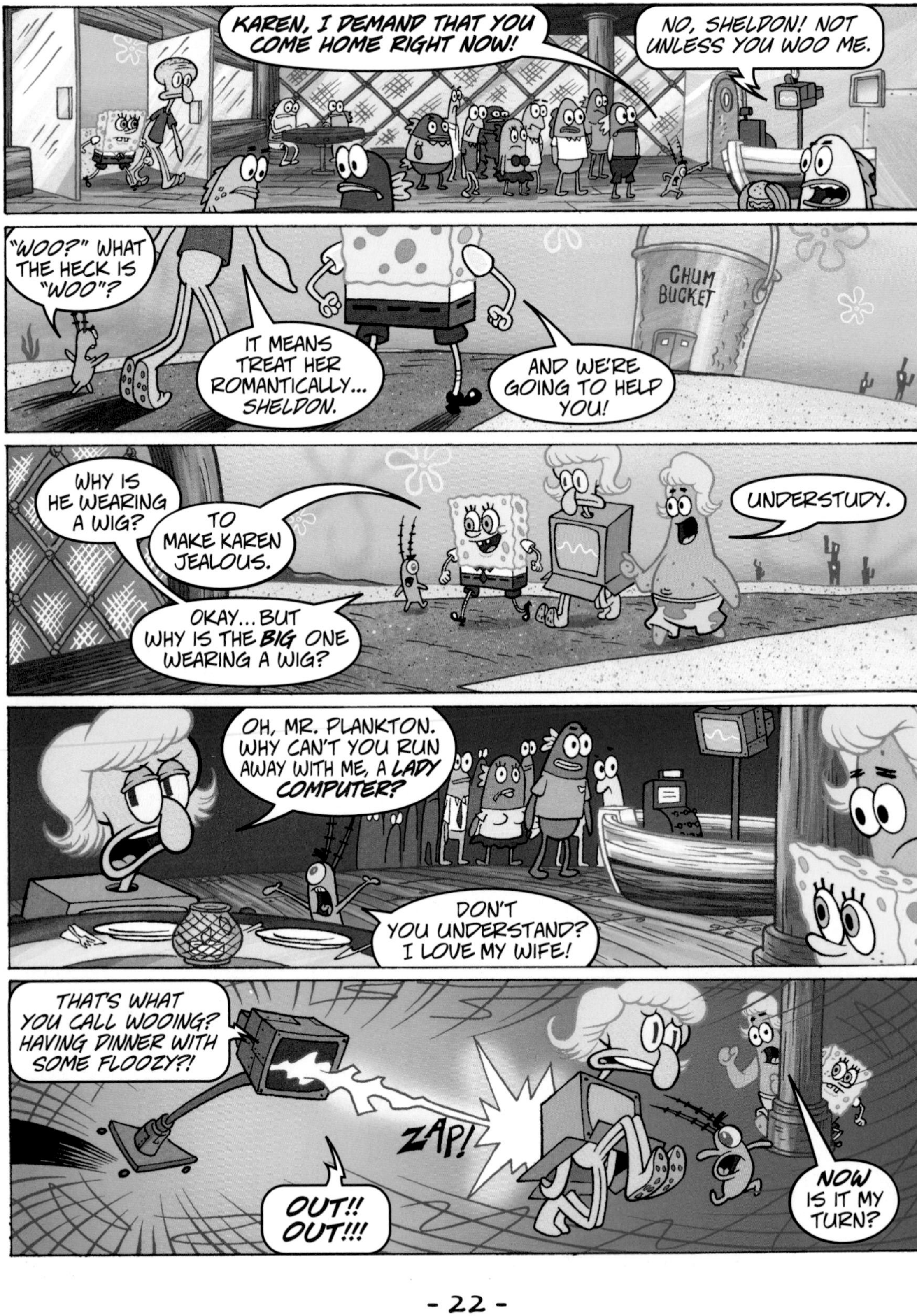
KAREN, I DEMAND THAT YOU COME HOME RIGHT NOW!
NO, SHELDON! NOT UNLESS YOU WOO ME.
"WOO?" WHAT THE HECK IS "WOO"?
IT MEANS TREAT HER ROMANTICALLY... SHELDON.
AND WE'RE GOING TO HELP YOU!
CHUM BUCKET
WHY IS HE WEARING A WIG?
TO MAKE KAREN JEALOUS.
OKAY... BUT WHY IS THE BIG ONE WEARING A WIG?
UNDERSTUDY.
OH, MR. PLANKTON. WHY CAN'T YOU RUN AWAY WITH ME, A LADY COMPUTER?
DON'T YOU UNDERSTAND? I LOVE MY WIFE!
THAT'S WHAT YOU CALL WOOING? HAVING DINNER WITH SOME FLOOZY?!
ZAP!
OUT!! OUT!!!
NOW IS IT MY TURN?

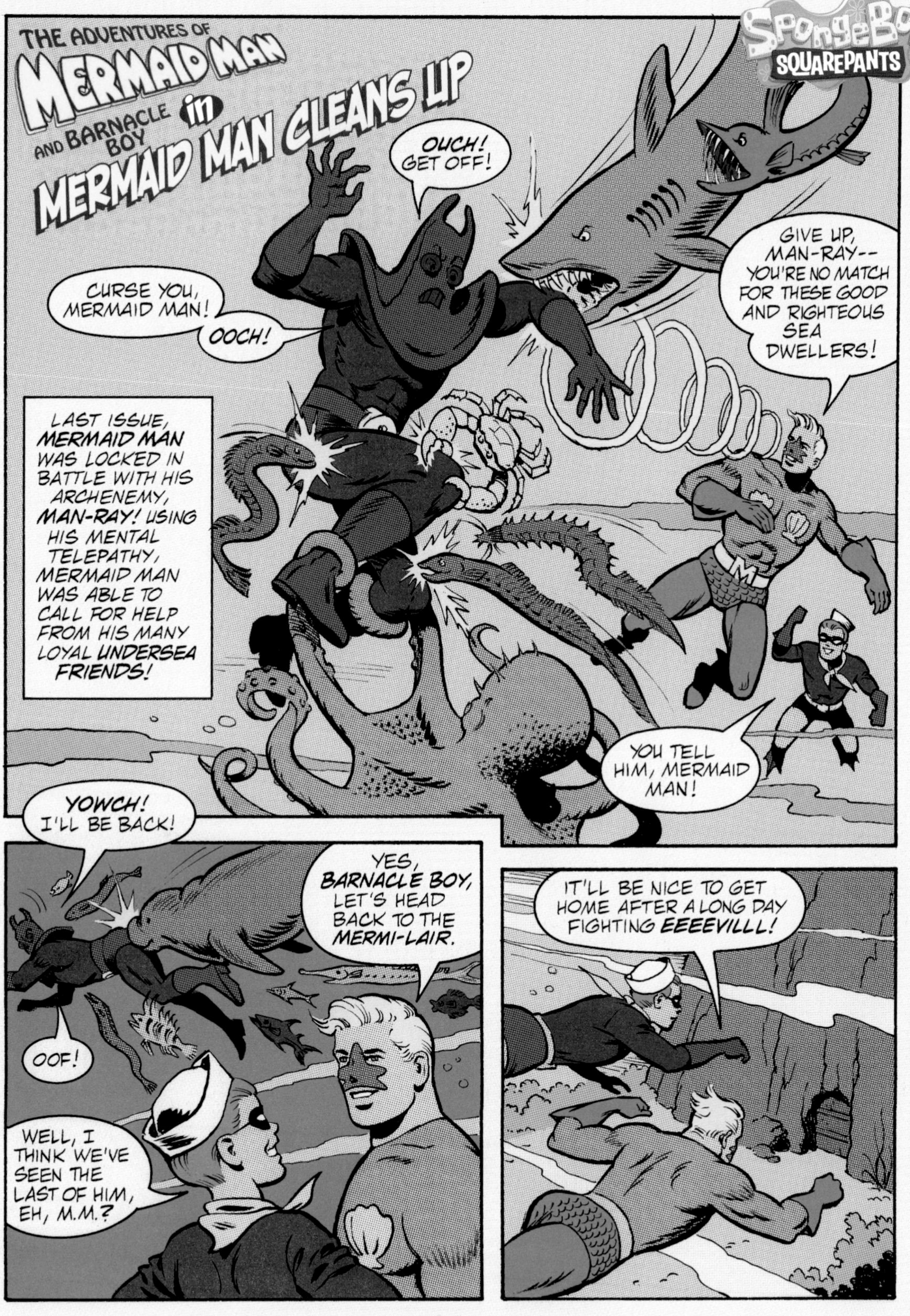
SpongeBob SQUAREPANTS
THE ADVENTURES OF MERMAID MAN AND BARNACLE BOY in MERMAID MAN CLEANS UP
OUCH! GET OFF!
CURSE YOU, MERMAID MAN!
OOCH!
GIVE UP, MAN-RAY-- YOU'RE NO MATCH FOR THESE GOOD AND RIGHTEOUS SEA DWELLERS!
LAST ISSUE, MERMAID MAN WAS LOCKED IN BATTLE WITH HIS ARCHENEMY, MAN-RAY! USING HIS MENTAL TELEPATHY, MERMAID MAN WAS ABLE TO CALL FOR HELP FROM HIS MANY LOYAL UNDERSEA FRIENDS!
YOU TELL HIM, MERMAID MAN!
YOWCH! I'LL BE BACK!
OOF!
WELL, I THINK WE'VE SEEN THE LAST OF HIM, EH, M.M.?
YES, BARNACLE BOY, LET'S HEAD BACK TO THE MERMI-LAIR.
IT'LL BE NICE TO GET HOME AFTER A LONG DAY FIGHTING EEEEVILLL!

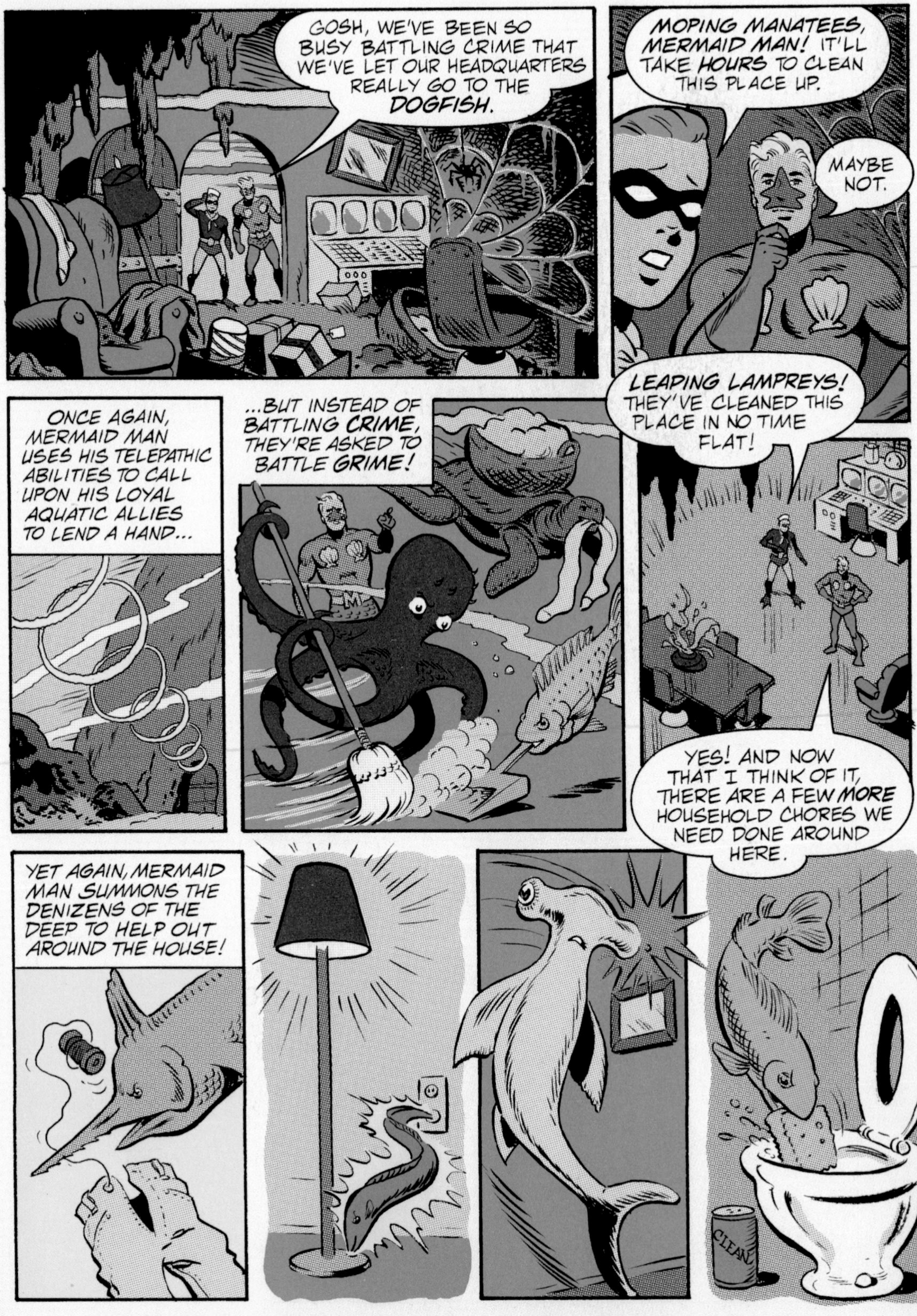
GOSH, WE'VE BEEN SO BUSY BATTLING CRIME THAT WE'VE LET OUR HEADQUARTERS REALLY GO TO THE DOGFISH.
MOPING MANATEES, MERMAID MAN! IT'LL TAKE HOURS TO CLEAN THIS PLACE UP.
MAYBE NOT.
ONCE AGAIN, MERMAID MAN USES HIS TELEPATHIC ABILITIES TO CALL UPON HIS LOYAL AQUATIC ALLIES TO LEND A HAND...
...BUT INSTEAD OF BATTLING CRIME, THEY'RE ASKED TO BATTLE GRIME!
LEAPING LAMPREYS! THEY'VE CLEANED THIS PLACE IN NO TIME FLAT!
YES! AND NOW THAT I THINK OF IT, THERE ARE A FEW MORE HOUSEHOLD CHORES WE NEED DONE AROUND HERE.
YET AGAIN, MERMAID MAN SUMMONS THE DENIZENS OF THE DEEP TO HELP OUT AROUND THE HOUSE!
CLEAN

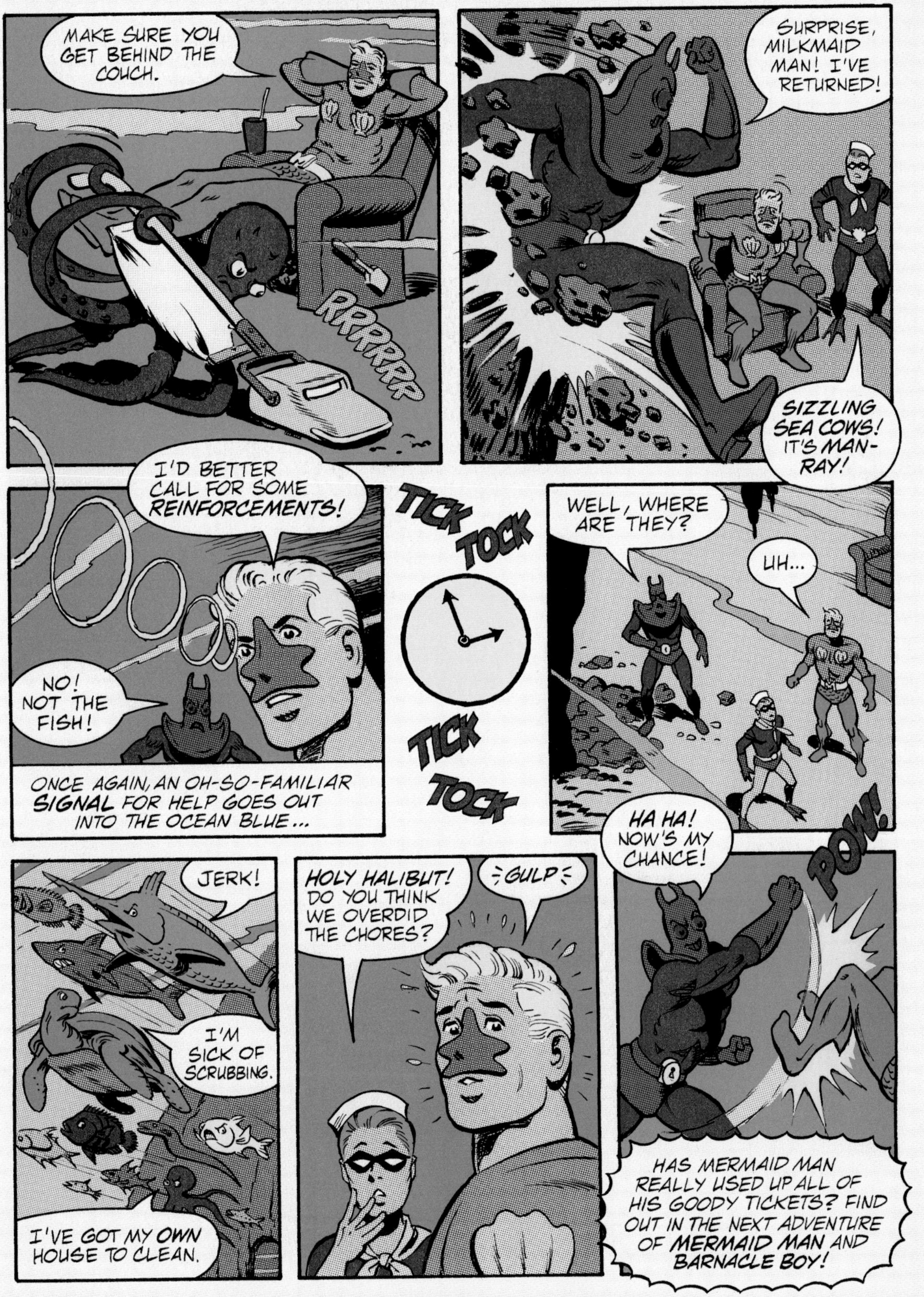

MAKE SURE YOU GET BEHIND THE COUCH.
RRRRRRR
SURPRISE, MILKMAID MAN! I'VE RETURNED!
SIZZLING SEA COWS! IT'S MAN-RAY!
I'D BETTER CALL FOR SOME REINFORCEMENTS!
NO! NOT THE FISH!
ONCE AGAIN, AN OH-SO-FAMILIAR SIGNAL FOR HELP GOES OUT INTO THE OCEAN BLUE...
TICK TOCK
TICK TOCK
WELL, WHERE ARE THEY?
UH...
JERK!
I'M SICK OF SCRUBBING.
I'VE GOT MY OWN HOUSE TO CLEAN.
HOLY HALIBUT! DO YOU THINK WE OVERDID THE CHORES?
GULP
HA HA! NOW'S MY CHANCE!
POW!
HAS MERMAID MAN REALLY USED UP ALL OF HIS GOODY TICKETS? FIND OUT IN THE NEXT ADVENTURE OF MERMAID MAN AND BARNACLE BOY!

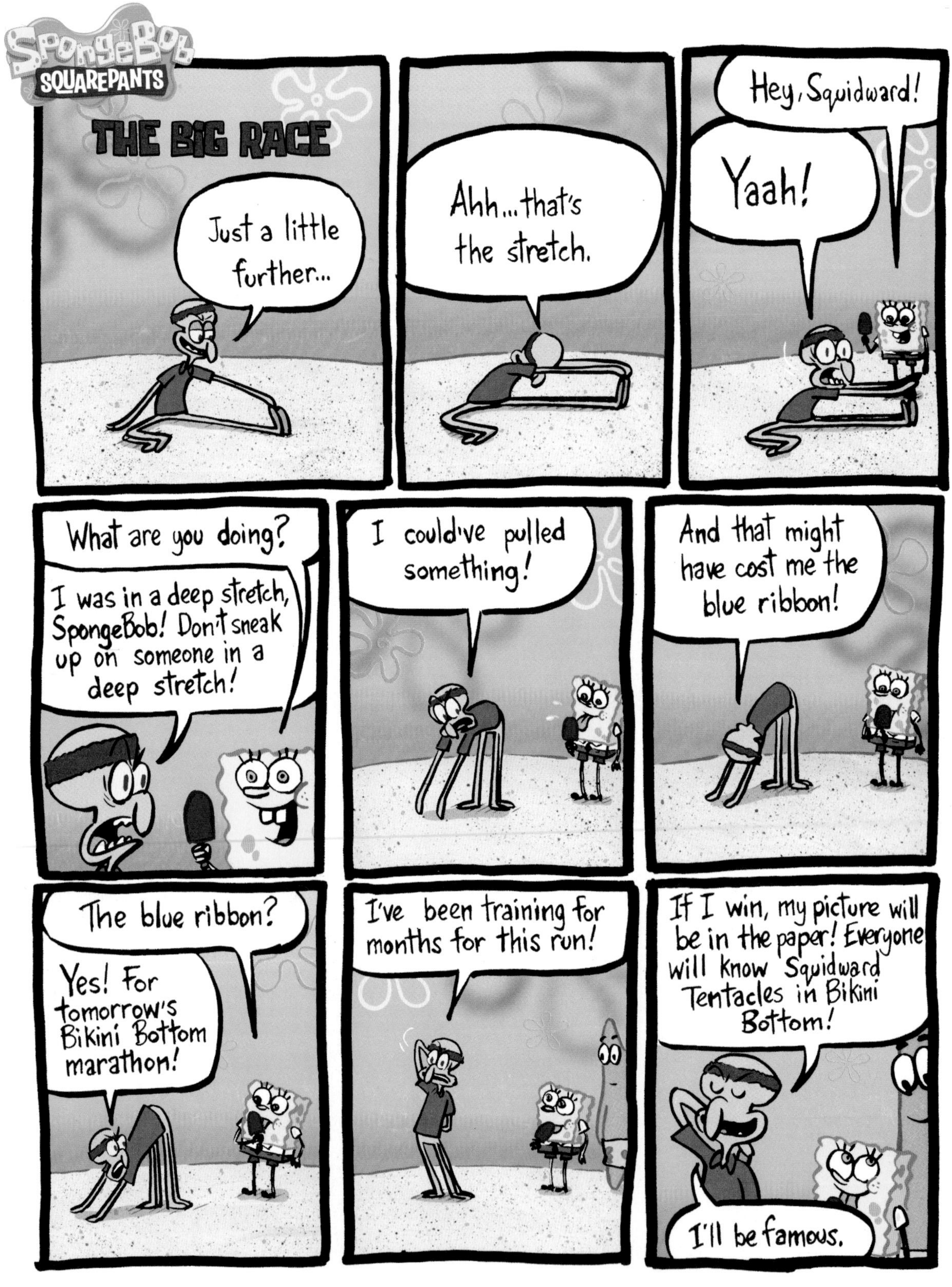
SpongeBob SquarePants
THE BIG RACE
Just a little further...
Ahh... that's the stretch.
Hey, Squidward!
Yaah!
What are you doing?
I was in a deep stretch, SpongeBob! Don't sneak up on someone in a deep stretch!
I could've pulled something!
And that might have cost me the blue ribbon!
The blue ribbon?
Yes! For tomorrow's Bikini Bottom marathon!
I've been training for months for this run!
If I win, my picture will be in the paper! Everyone will know Squidward Tentacles in Bikini Bottom!
I'll be famous.

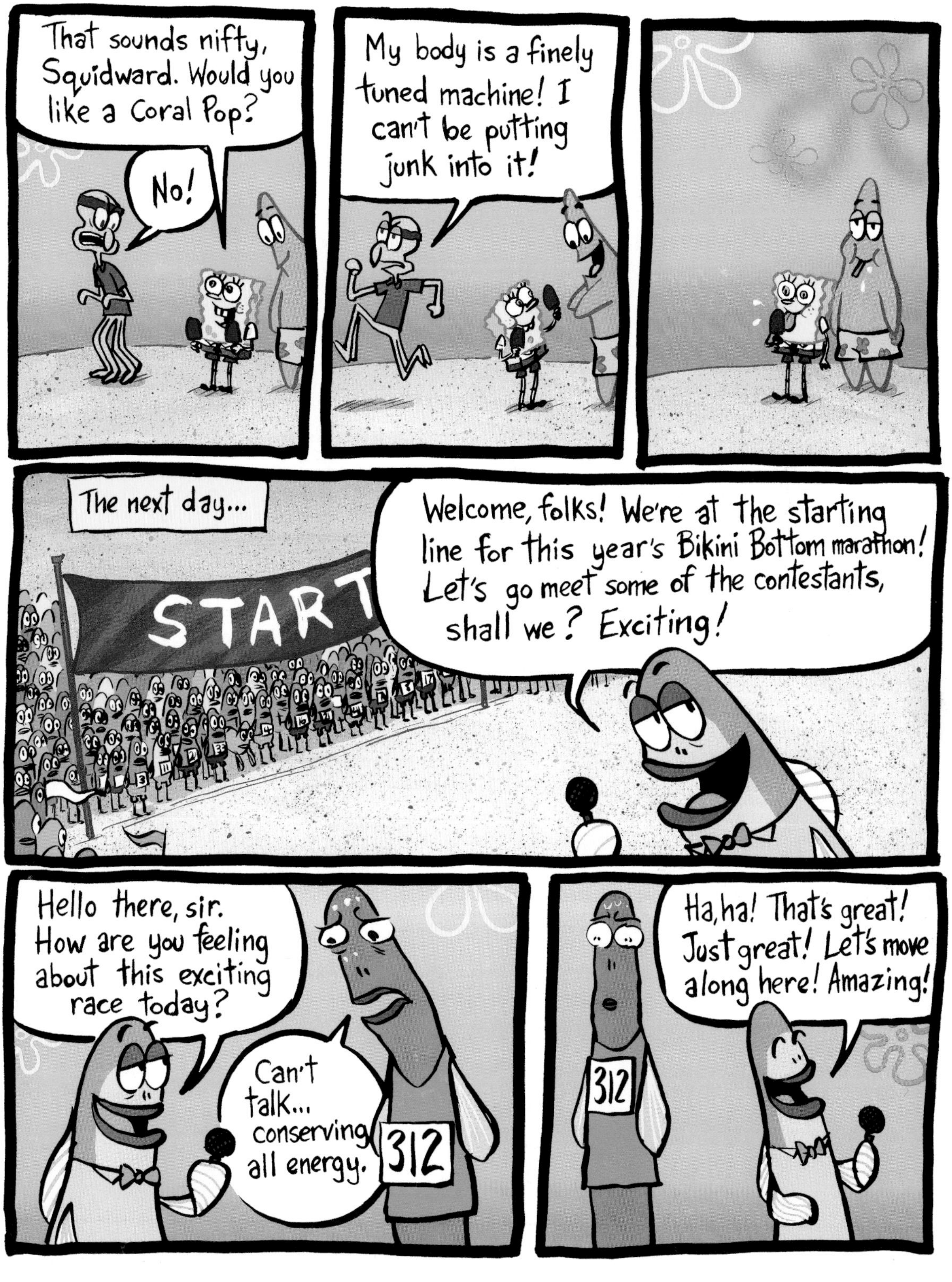
That sounds nifty, Squidward. Would you like a Coral Pop?
No!
My body is a finely tuned machine! I can't be putting junk into it!
The next day...
Welcome, folks! We're at the starting line for this year's Bikini Bottom marathon! Let's go meet some of the contestants, shall we? Exciting!
START
Hello there, sir. How are you feeling about this exciting race today?
Can't talk... conserving all energy.
312
312
Ha, ha! That's great! Just great! Let's move along here! Amazing!

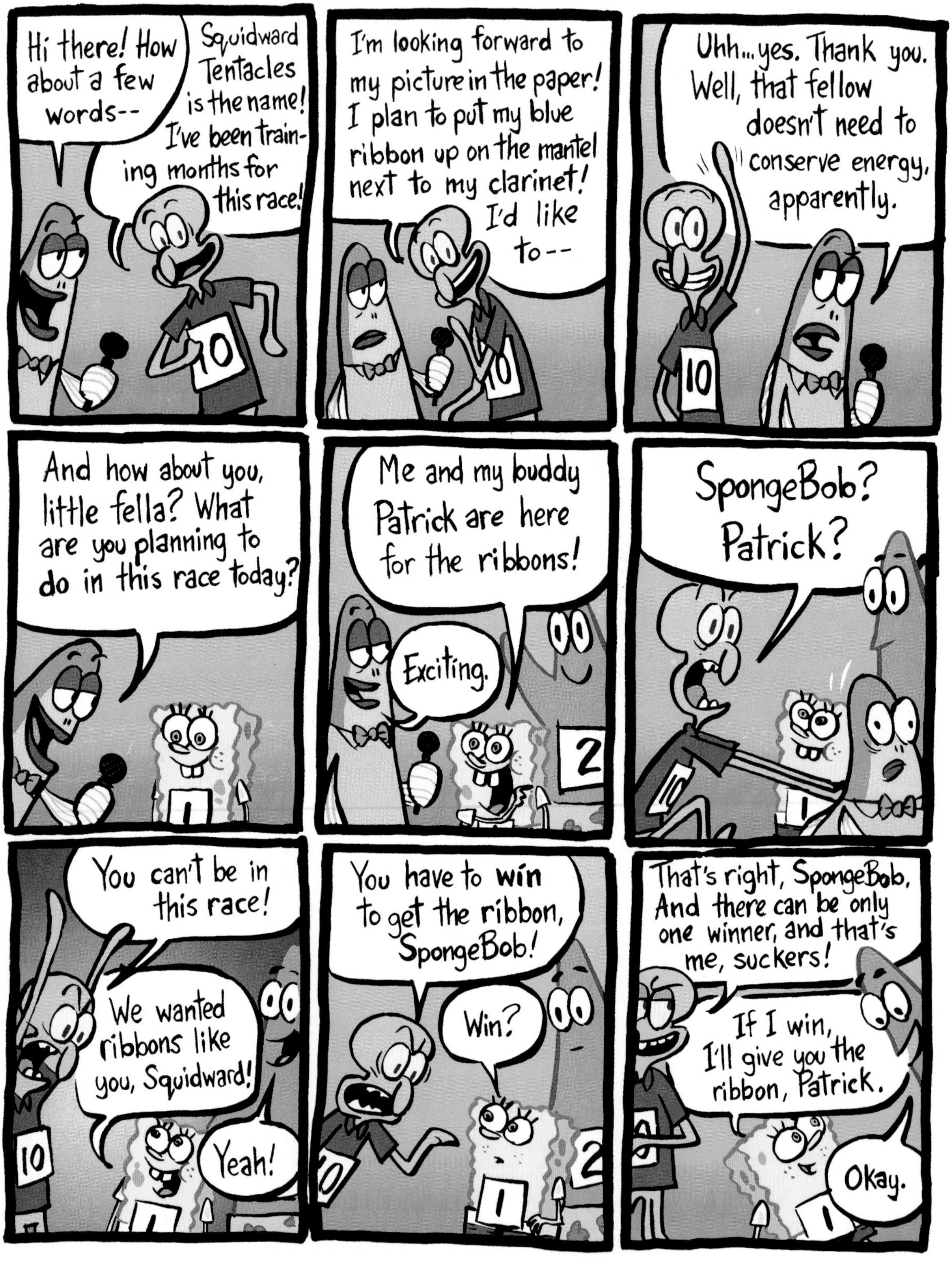
Hi there! How about a few words--
Squidward Tentacles is the name! I've been training months for this race!
I'm looking forward to my picture in the paper! I plan to put my blue ribbon up on the mantel next to my clarinet!
I'd like to--
Uhh... yes. Thank you. Well, that fellow doesn't need to conserve energy, apparently.
10
And how about you, little fella? What are you planning to do in this race today?
Me and my buddy Patrick are here for the ribbons!
Exciting.
2
SpongeBob? Patrick?
You can't be in this race!
We wanted ribbons like you, Squidward!
Yeah!
10
You have to **win** to get the ribbon, SpongeBob!
Win?
That's right, SpongeBob. And there can be only one winner, and that's me, suckers!
If I win, I'll give you the ribbon, Patrick.
Okay.

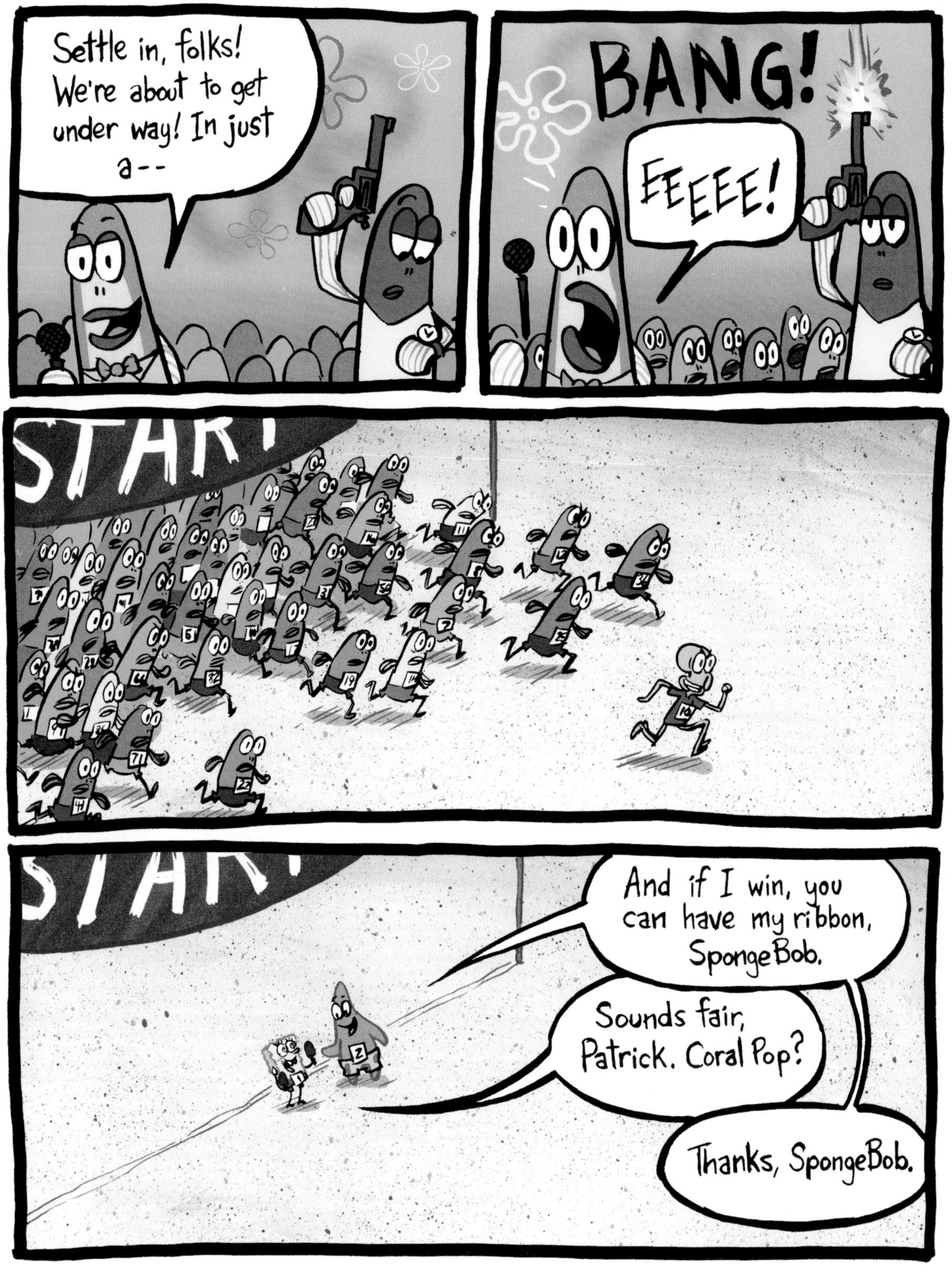
Settle in, folks! We're about to get under way! In just a--
BANG!
EEEEE!
START
START
And if I win, you can have my ribbon, SpongeBob.
Sounds fair, Patrick. Coral Pop?
Thanks, SpongeBob.

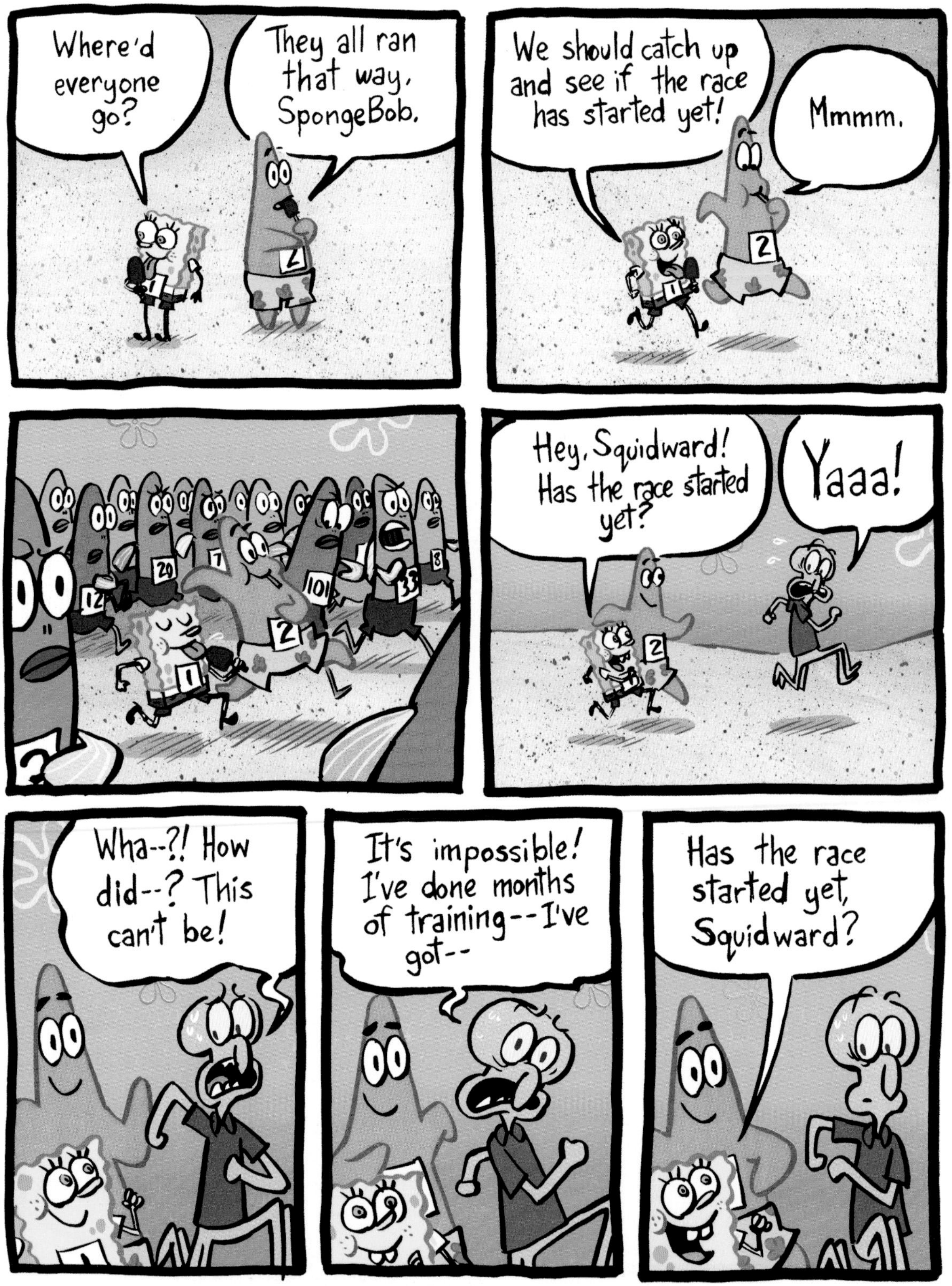
Where'd everyone go?
They all ran that way, SpongeBob.
We should catch up and see if the race has started yet!
Mmmm.
1
2
20
7
12
101
33
8
2
1
Hey, Squidward! Has the race started yet?
Yaaa!
2
Wha--?! How did--? This can't be!
It's impossible! I've done months of training--I've got--
Has the race started yet, Squidward?

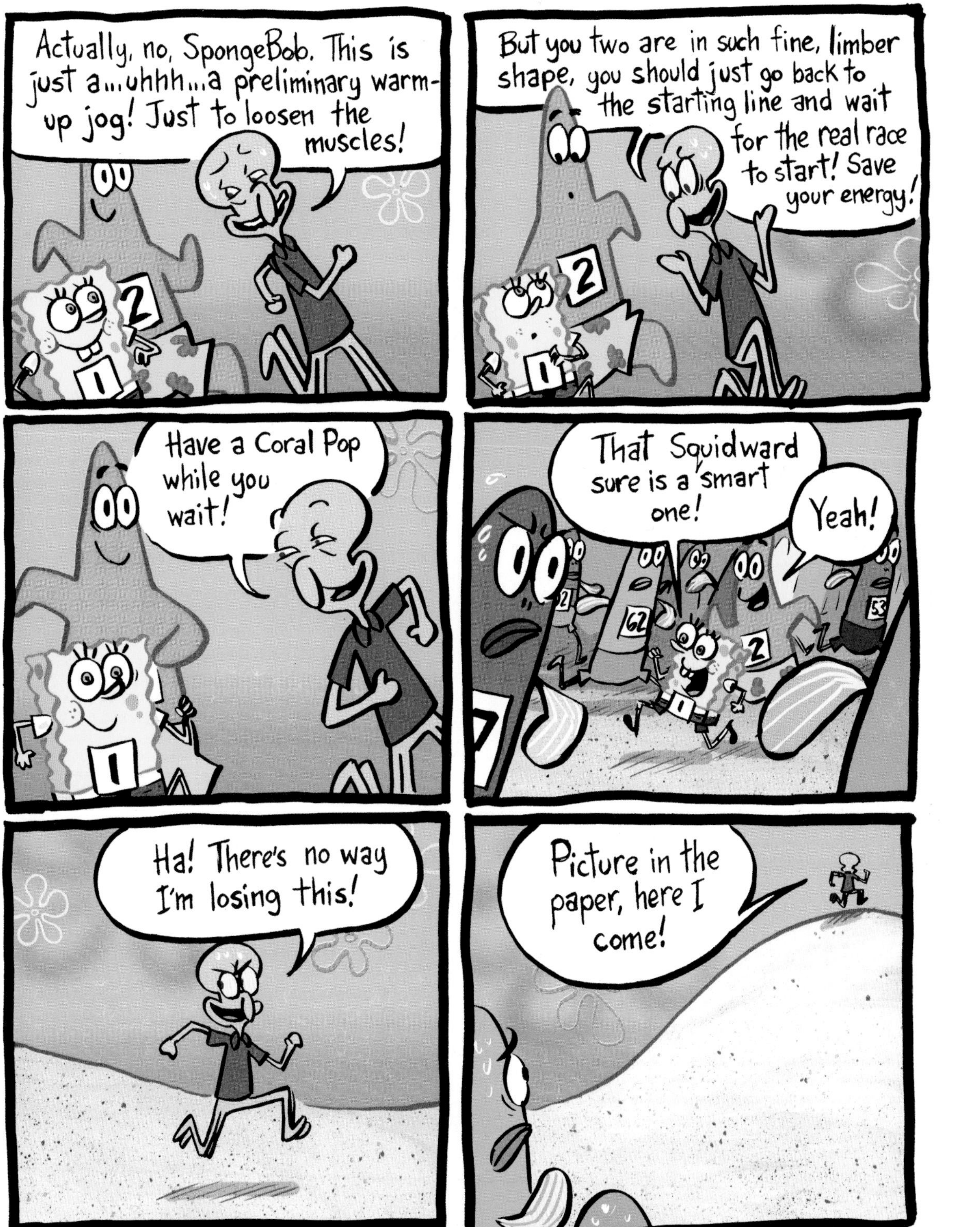
Actually, no, SpongeBob. This is just a...uhhh...a preliminary warm-up jog! Just to loosen the muscles!
But you two are in such fine, limber shape, you should just go back to the starting line and wait for the real race to start! Save your energy!
Have a Coral Pop while you wait!
That Squidward sure is a smart one!
Yeah!
Ha! There's no way I'm losing this!
Picture in the paper, here I come!

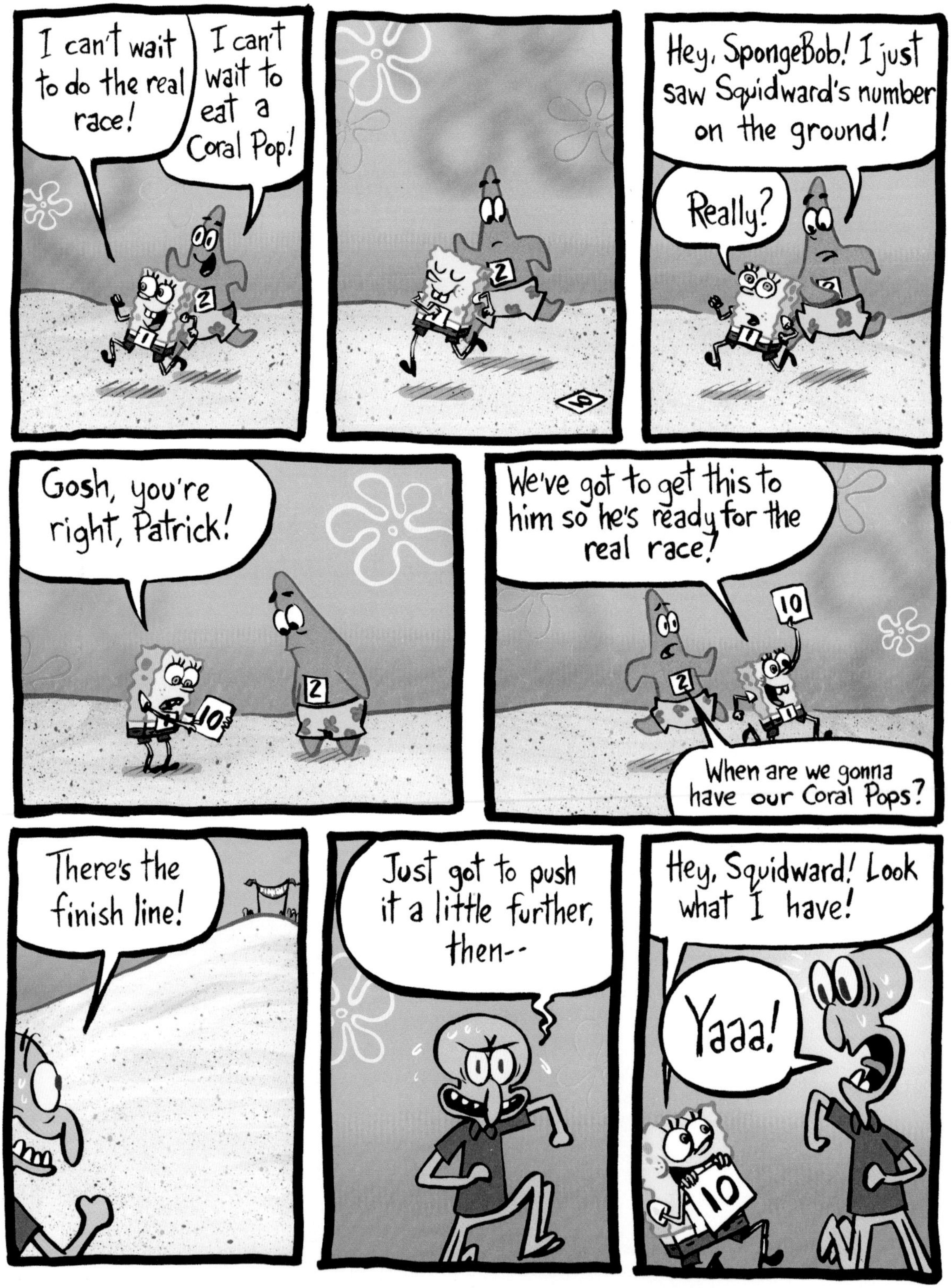
I can't wait to do the real race!
I can't wait to eat a Coral Pop!
Hey, SpongeBob! I just saw Squidward's number on the ground!
Really?
Gosh, you're right, Patrick!
We've got to get this to him so he's ready for the real race!
When are we gonna have our Coral Pops?
There's the finish line!
Just got to push it a little further, then--
Hey, Squidward! Look what I have!
Yaaa!

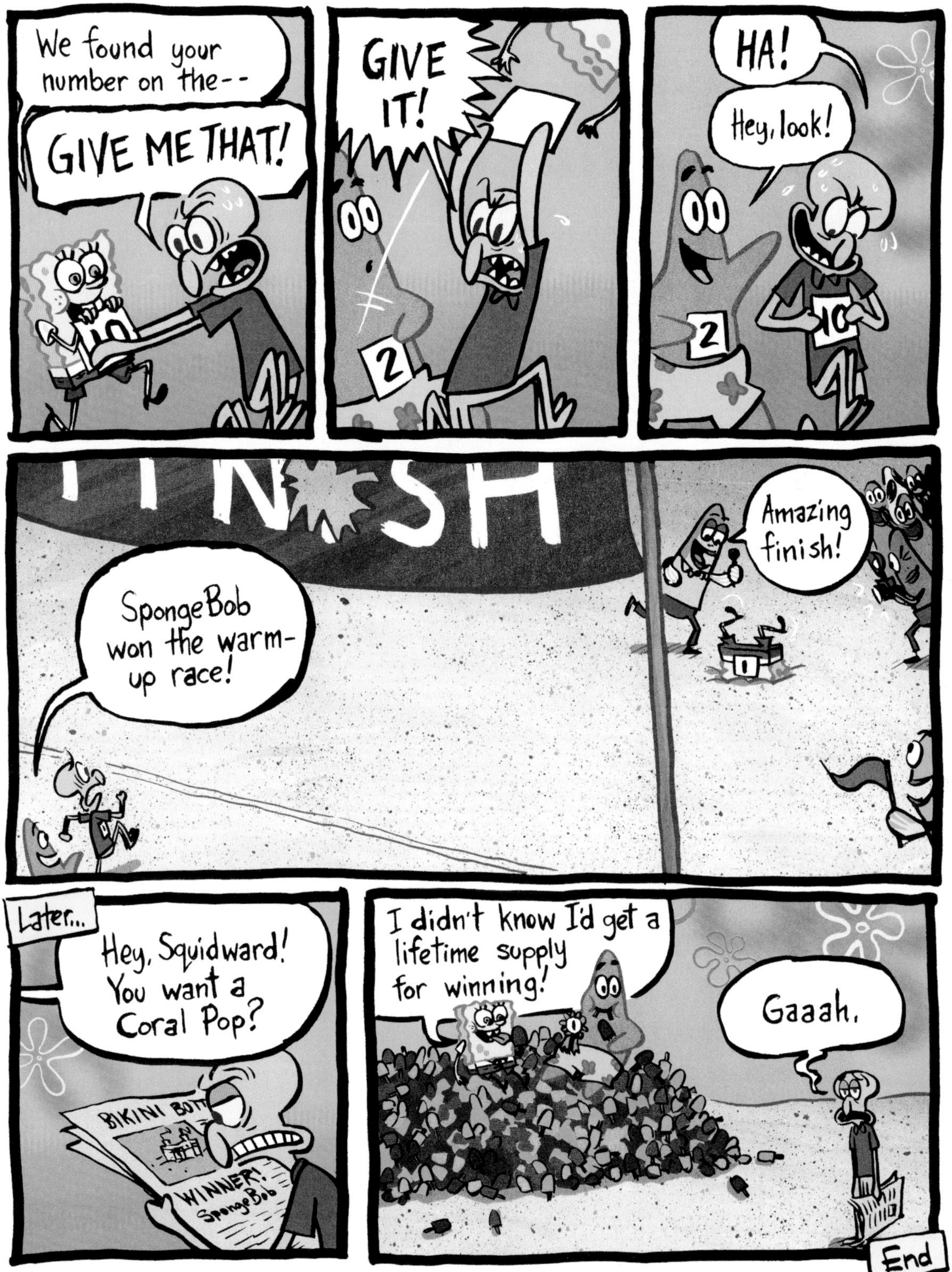

We found your number on the--
GIVE ME THAT!
GIVE IT!
HA!
Hey, look!
FINISH
SpongeBob won the warm-up race!
Amazing finish!
Later...
Hey, Squidward! You want a Coral Pop?
WINNER! SpongeBob
I didn't know I'd get a lifetime supply for winning!
Gaaah.
End

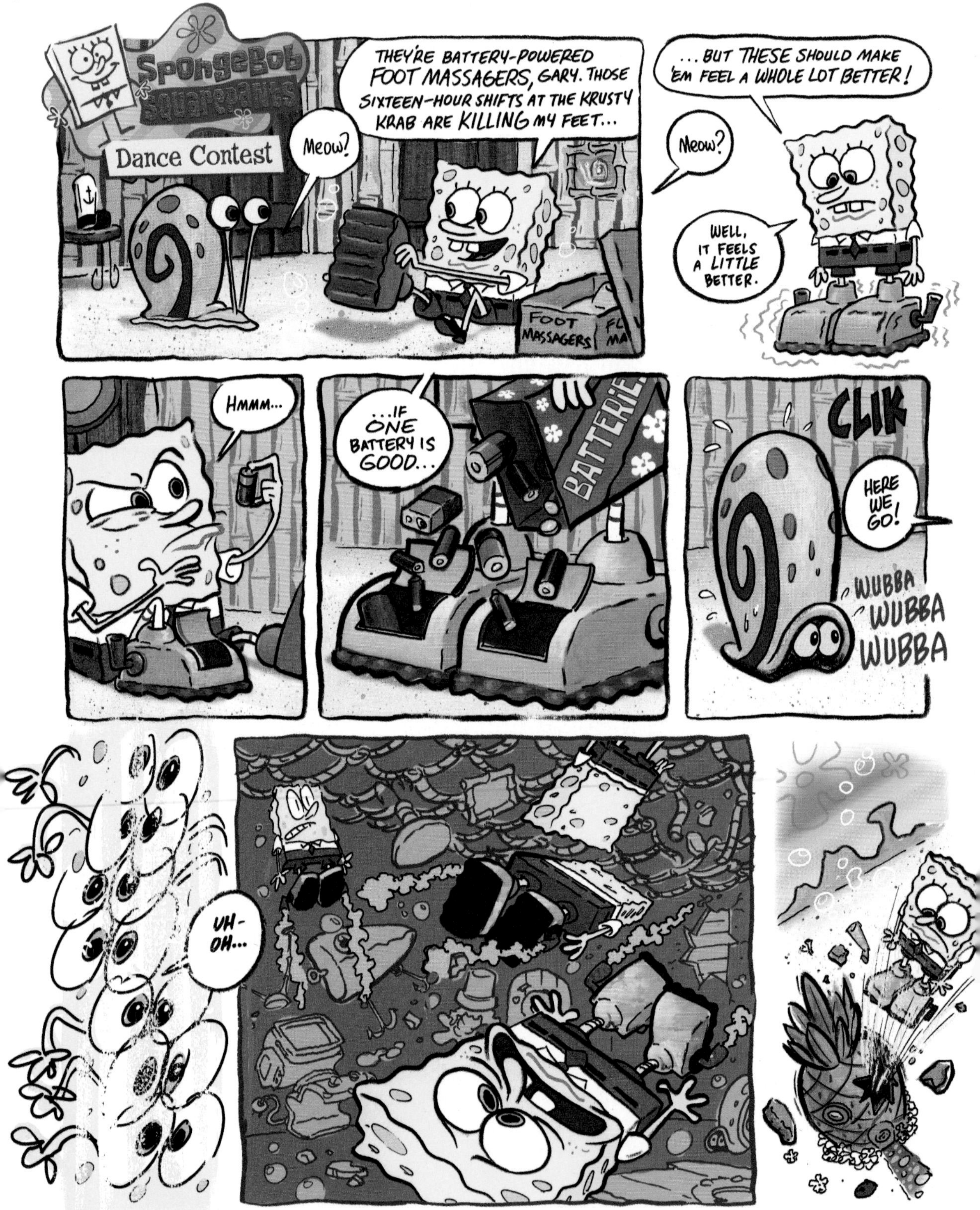
SpongeBob SquarePants
Dance Contest
Meow?
THEY'RE BATTERY-POWERED FOOT MASSAGERS, GARY. THOSE SIXTEEN-HOUR SHIFTS AT THE KRUSTY KRAB ARE KILLING MY FEET...
FOOT MASSAGERS
Meow?
... BUT THESE SHOULD MAKE 'EM FEEL A WHOLE LOT BETTER!
WELL, IT FEELS A LITTLE BETTER.
HMMM...
...IF ONE BATTERY IS GOOD...
BATTERIES
CLIK
HERE WE GO!
WUBBA WUBBA WUBBA
UH-OH...

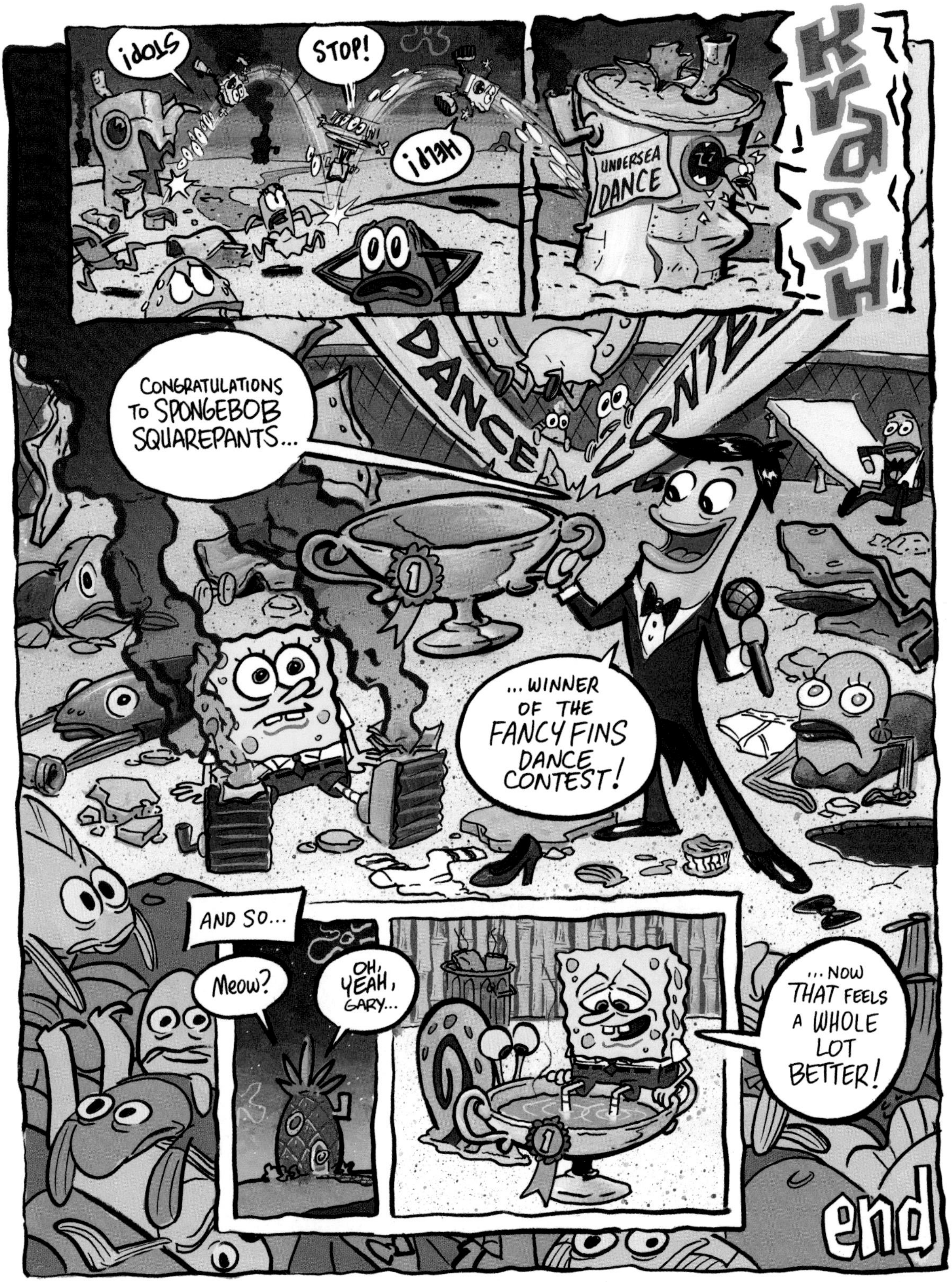

STOP!
STOP!
HELP!
UNDERSEA DANCE
KRASH
DANCE
CONGRATULATIONS TO SPONGEBOB SQUAREPANTS...
...WINNER OF THE FANCY FINS DANCE CONTEST!
AND SO...
Meow?
OH, YEAH, GARY...
...NOW THAT FEELS A WHOLE LOT BETTER!
end

SpongeBob SquarePants

STARING CONTEST

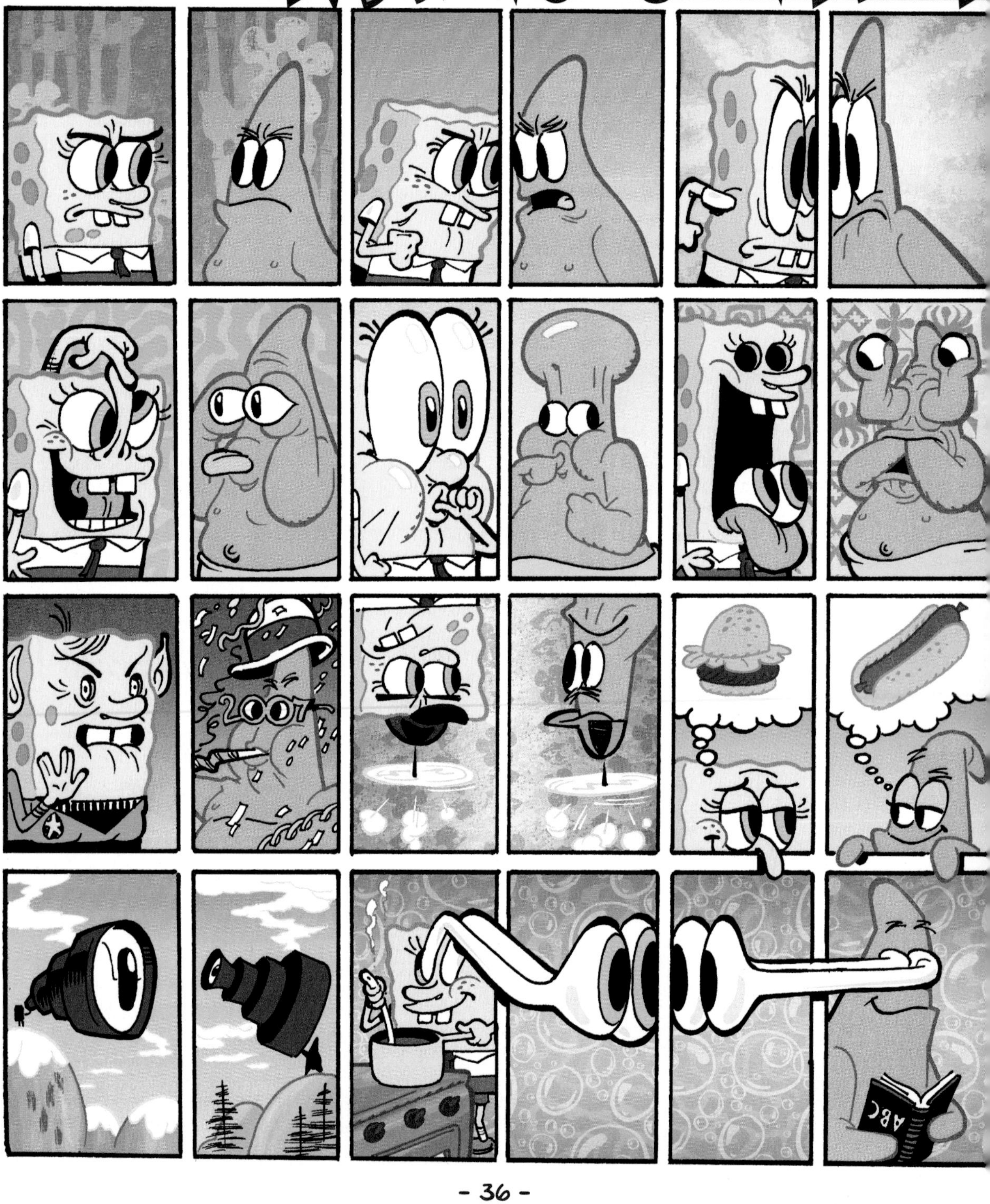

2007
ABC

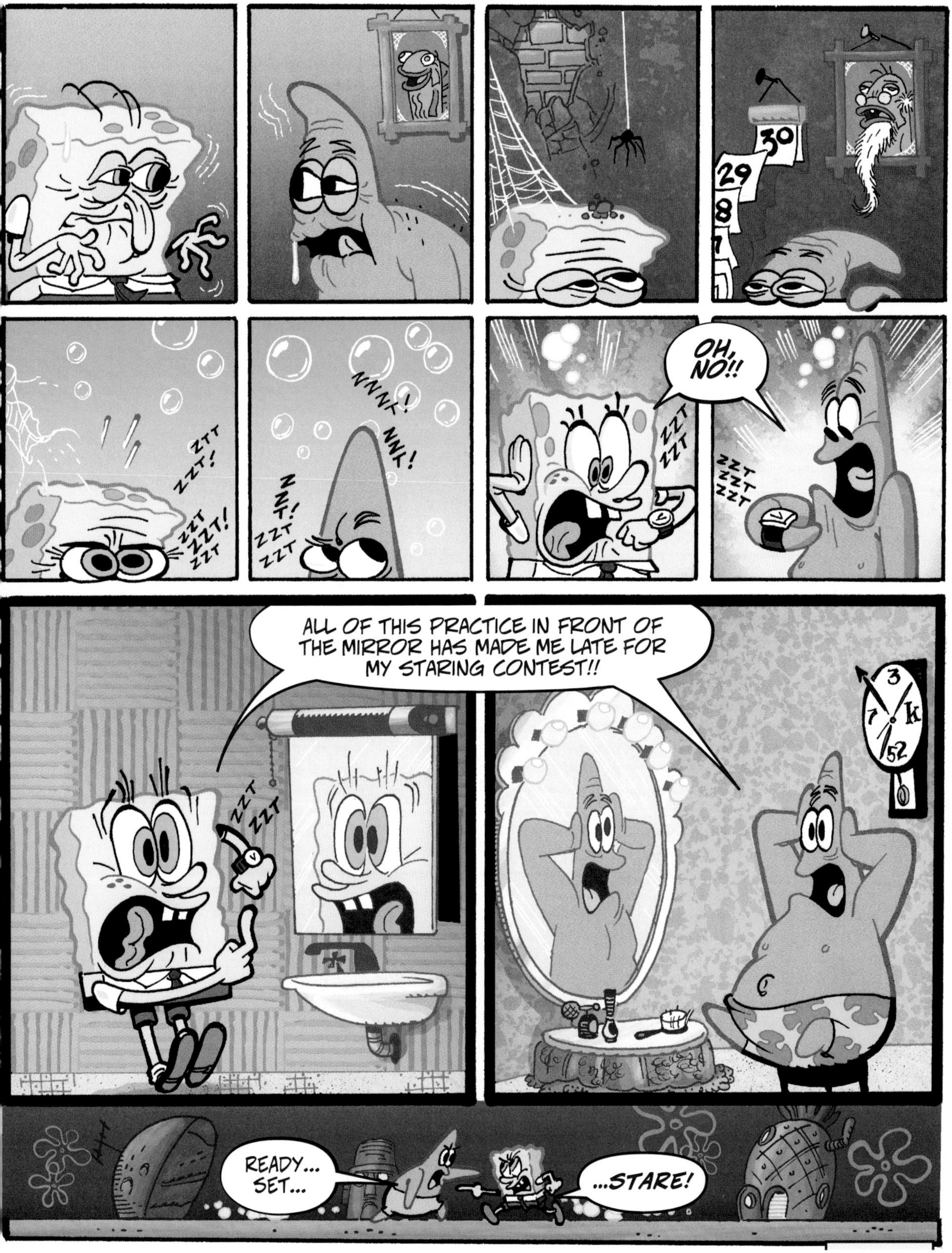
30
29
8
ZZT
ZZT!
ZZT
ZZT!
ZZT
NNNT!
NNT!
Z
ZT!
ZZT
ZZT
OH, NO!!
ZZT
ZZT
ZZT
ZZT
ZZT
ALL OF THIS PRACTICE IN FRONT OF THE MIRROR HAS MADE ME LATE FOR MY STARING CONTEST!!
ZZT
ZZT
READY... SET...
...STARE!

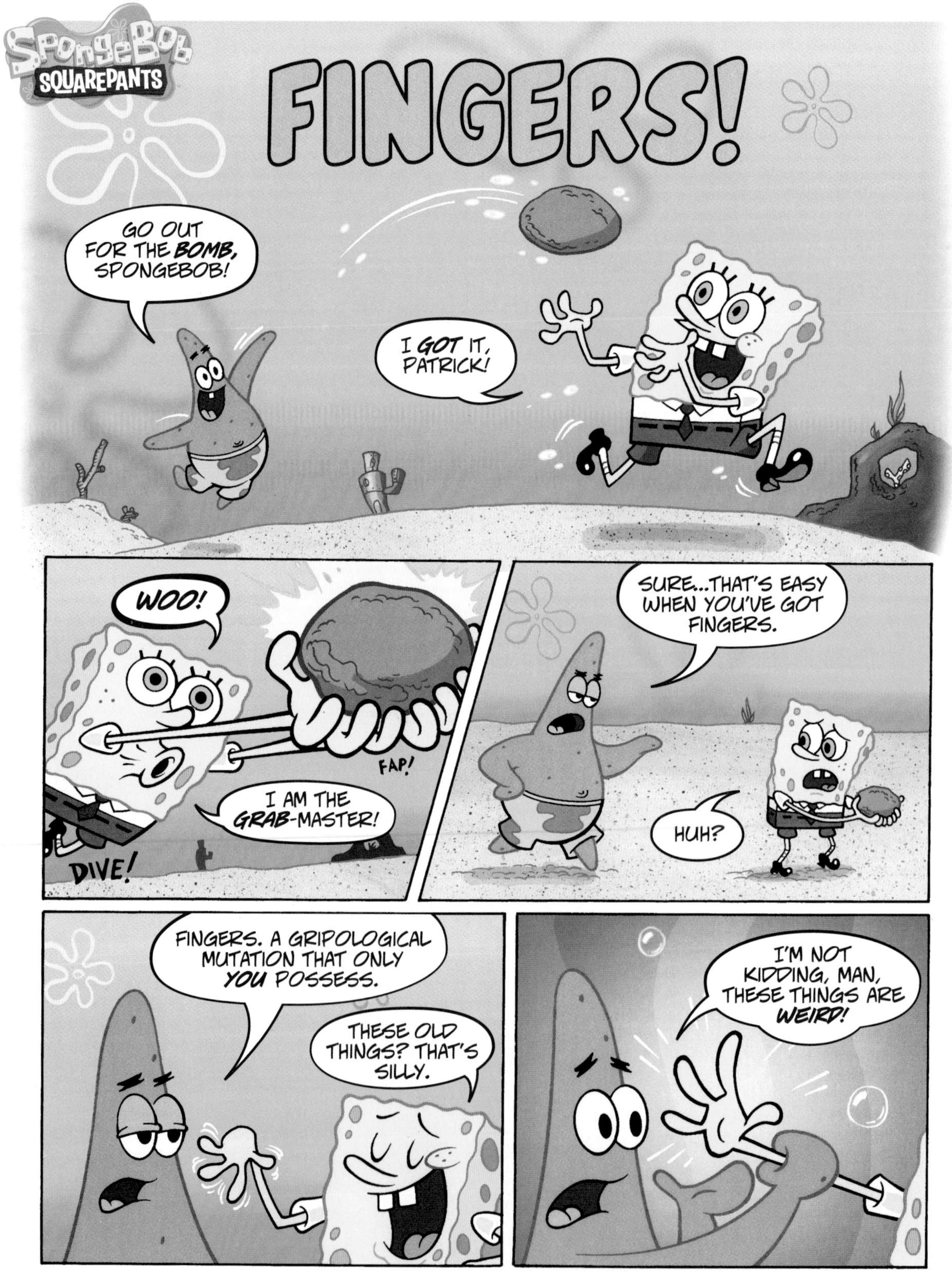
SpongeBob SQUAREPANTS
FINGERS!
GO OUT FOR THE BOMB, SPONGEBOB!
I GOT IT, PATRICK!
WOO!
I AM THE GRAB-MASTER!
FAP!
DIVE!
SURE...THAT'S EASY WHEN YOU'VE GOT FINGERS.
HUH?
FINGERS. A GRIPOLOGICAL MUTATION THAT ONLY YOU POSSESS.
THESE OLD THINGS? THAT'S SILLY.
I'M NOT KIDDING, MAN, THESE THINGS ARE WEIRD!

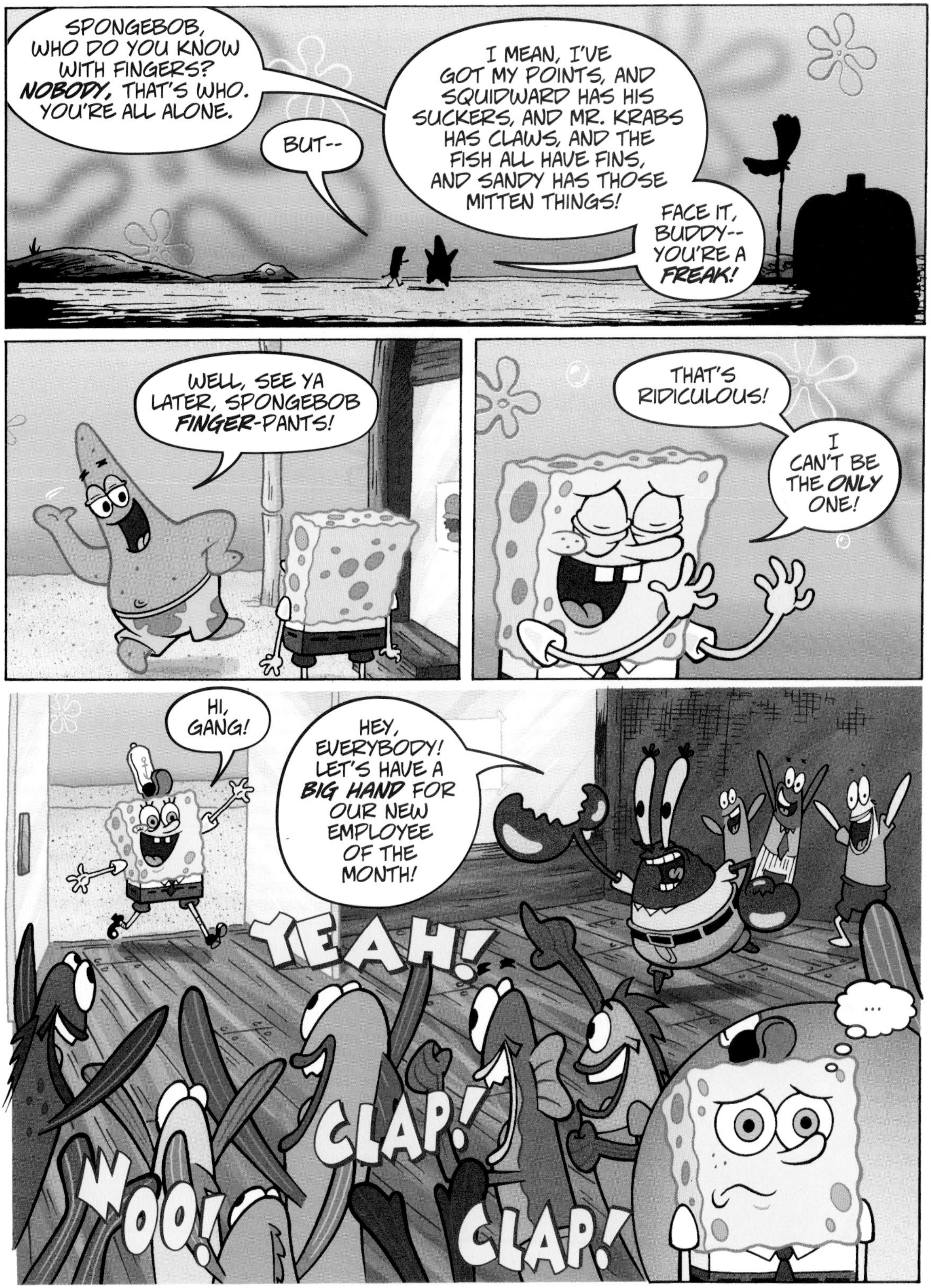
SPONGEBOB, WHO DO YOU KNOW WITH FINGERS? NOBODY, THAT'S WHO. YOU'RE ALL ALONE.
BUT--
I MEAN, I'VE GOT MY POINTS, AND SQUIDWARD HAS HIS SUCKERS, AND MR. KRABS HAS CLAWS, AND THE FISH ALL HAVE FINS, AND SANDY HAS THOSE MITTEN THINGS!
FACE IT, BUDDY-- YOU'RE A FREAK!
WELL, SEE YA LATER, SPONGEBOB FINGER-PANTS!
THAT'S RIDICULOUS!
I CAN'T BE THE ONLY ONE!
HI, GANG!
HEY, EVERYBODY! LET'S HAVE A BIG HAND FOR OUR NEW EMPLOYEE OF THE MONTH!
YEAH!
CLAP!
WOO!
CLAP!
...

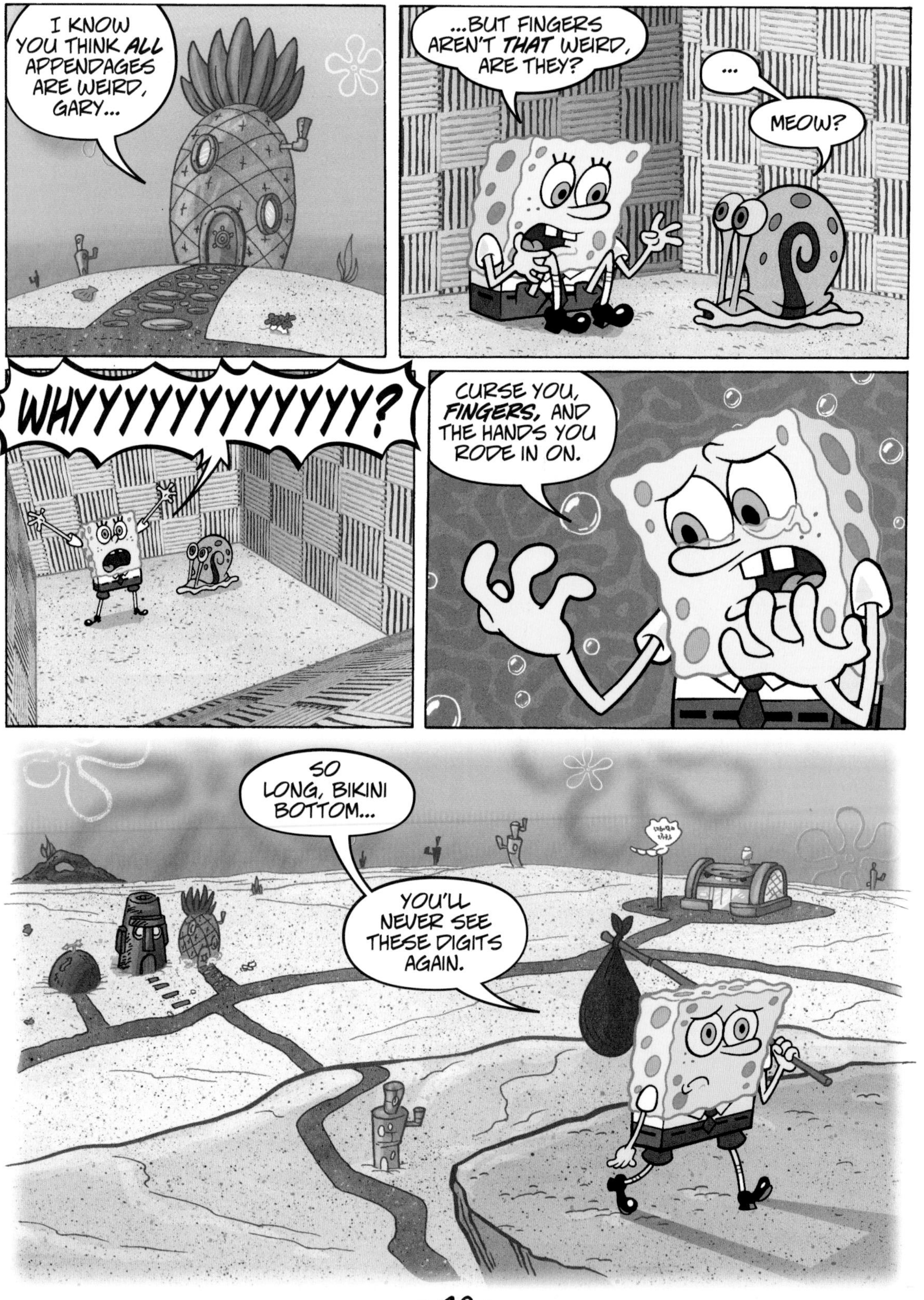
I KNOW YOU THINK ALL APPENDAGES ARE WEIRD, GARY...
...BUT FINGERS AREN'T THAT WEIRD, ARE THEY?
...
MEOW?
WHYYYYYYYYYYYYY?
CURSE YOU, FINGERS, AND THE HANDS YOU RODE IN ON.
SO LONG, BIKINI BOTTOM...
YOU'LL NEVER SEE THESE DIGITS AGAIN.

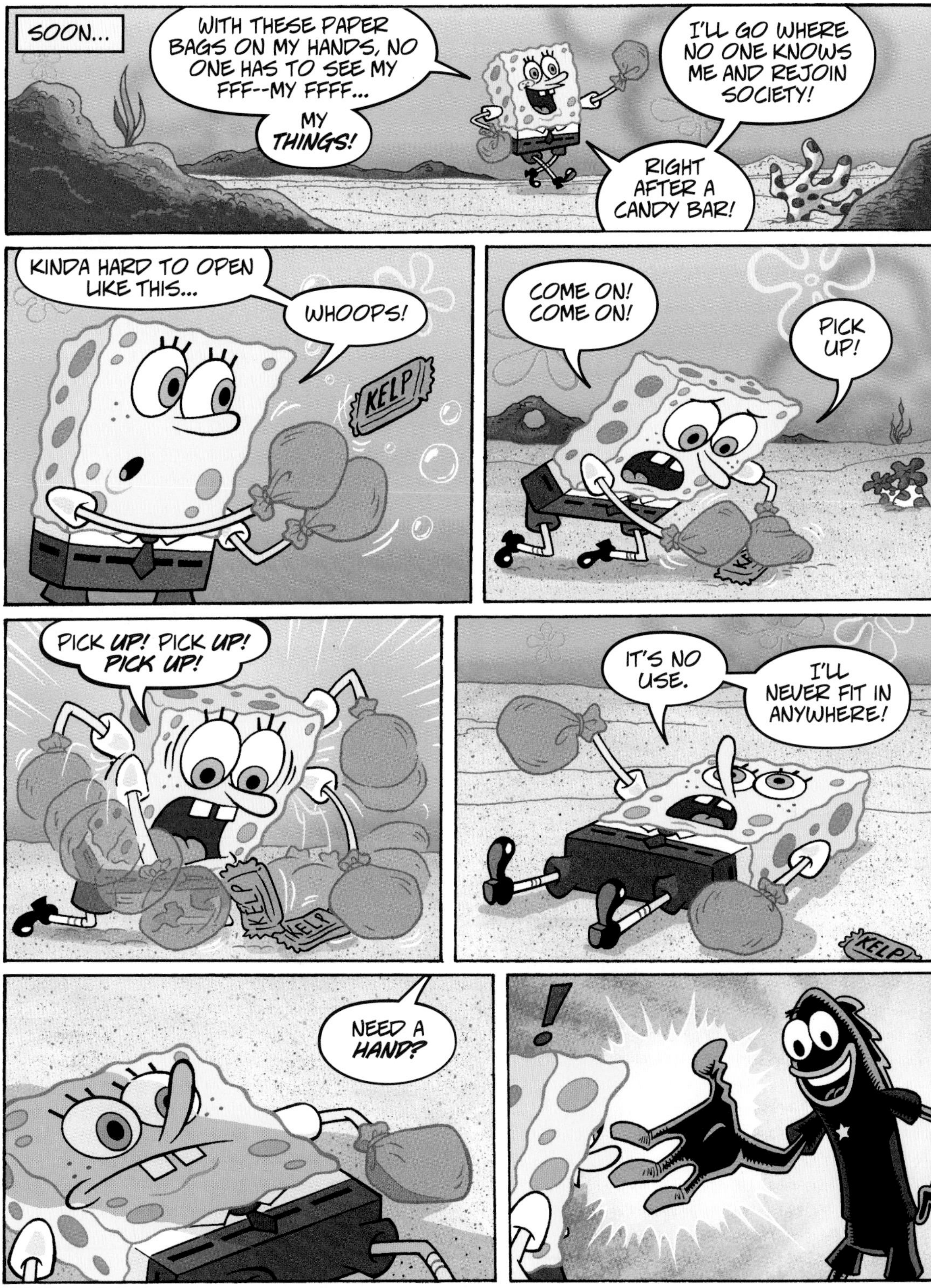
SOON...
WITH THESE PAPER BAGS ON MY HANDS, NO ONE HAS TO SEE MY FFF--MY FFFF...
MY *THINGS!*
I'LL GO WHERE NO ONE KNOWS ME AND REJOIN SOCIETY!
RIGHT AFTER A CANDY BAR!
KINDA HARD TO OPEN LIKE THIS...
WHOOPS!
KELP
COME ON! COME ON!
PICK UP!
PICK *UP!* PICK *UP!* ***PICK UP!***
KELP
IT'S NO USE.
I'LL NEVER FIT IN ANYWHERE!
KELP
NEED A *HAND?*
!

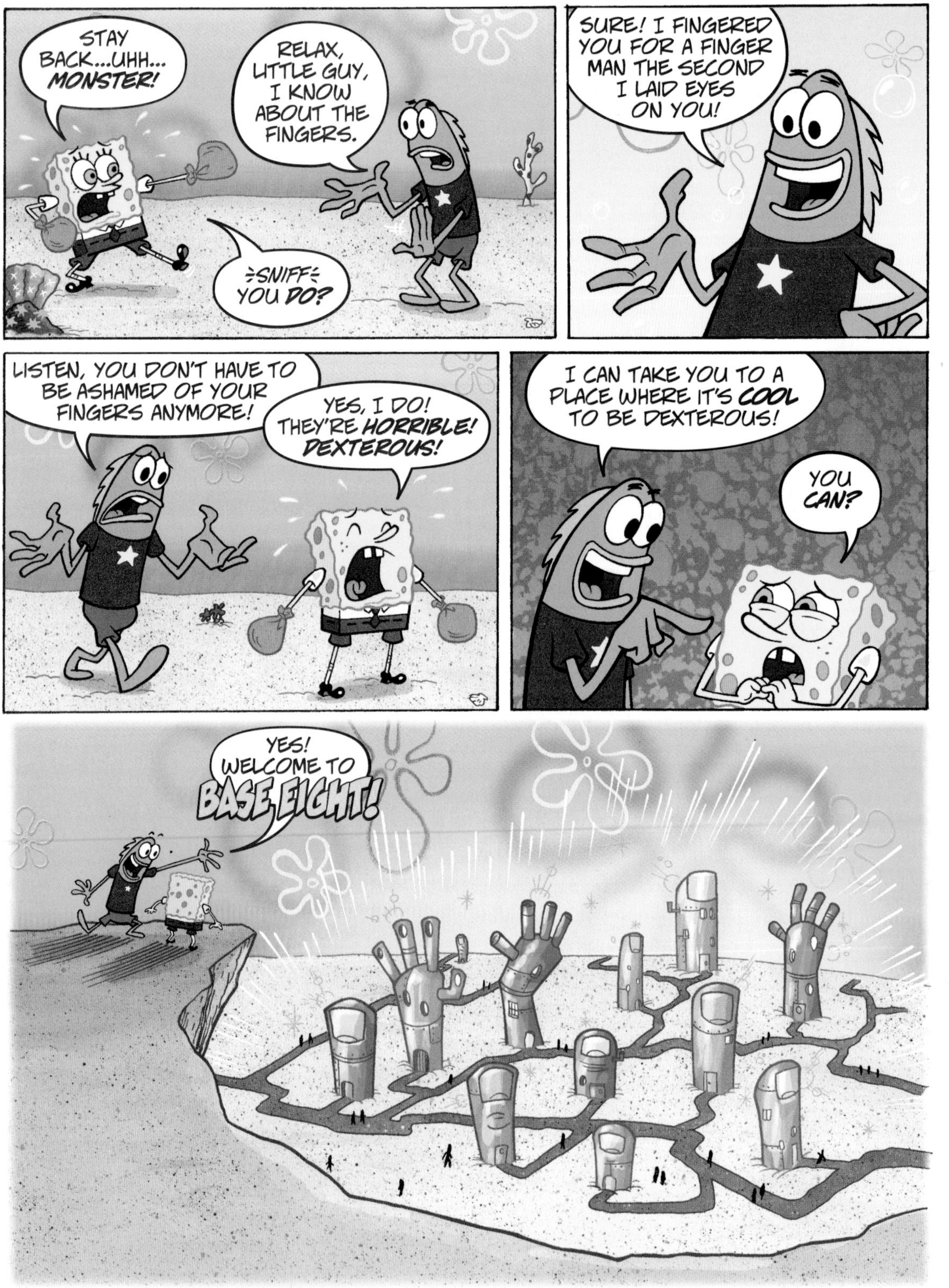
STAY BACK...UHH... MONSTER!
RELAX, LITTLE GUY, I KNOW ABOUT THE FINGERS.
≠SNIFF≠ YOU DO?
SURE! I FINGERED YOU FOR A FINGER MAN THE SECOND I LAID EYES ON YOU!
LISTEN, YOU DON'T HAVE TO BE ASHAMED OF YOUR FINGERS ANYMORE!
YES, I DO! THEY'RE HORRIBLE! DEXTEROUS!
I CAN TAKE YOU TO A PLACE WHERE IT'S COOL TO BE DEXTEROUS!
YOU CAN?
YES! WELCOME TO BASE EIGHT!

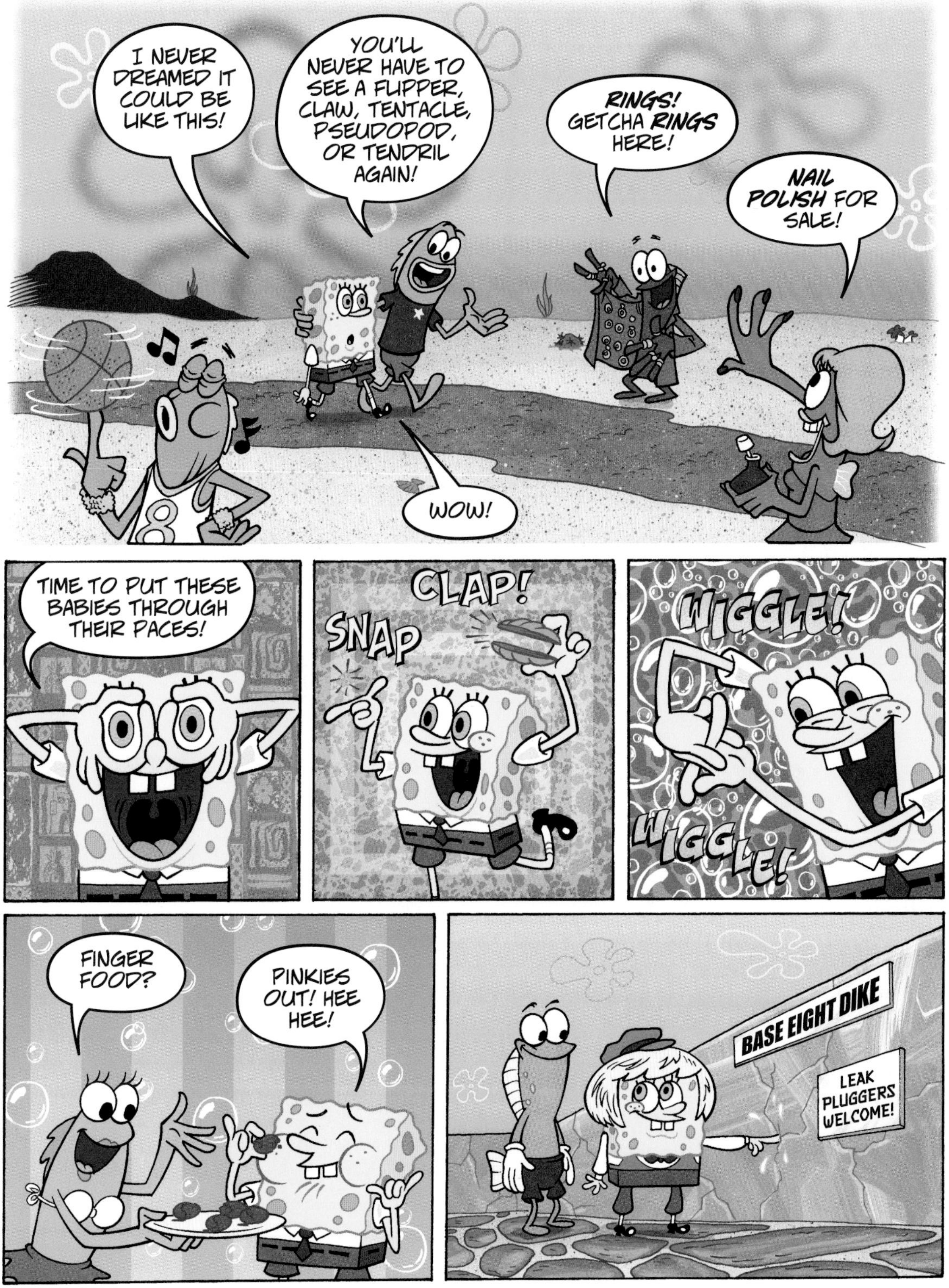
I NEVER DREAMED IT COULD BE LIKE THIS!
YOU'LL NEVER HAVE TO SEE A FLIPPER, CLAW, TENTACLE, PSEUDOPOD, OR TENDRIL AGAIN!
RINGS! GETCHA RINGS HERE!
NAIL POLISH FOR SALE!
WOW!
TIME TO PUT THESE BABIES THROUGH THEIR PACES!
CLAP!
SNAP
WIGGLE!
WIGGLE!
FINGER FOOD?
PINKIES OUT! HEE HEE!
BASE EIGHT DIKE
LEAK PLUGGERS WELCOME!

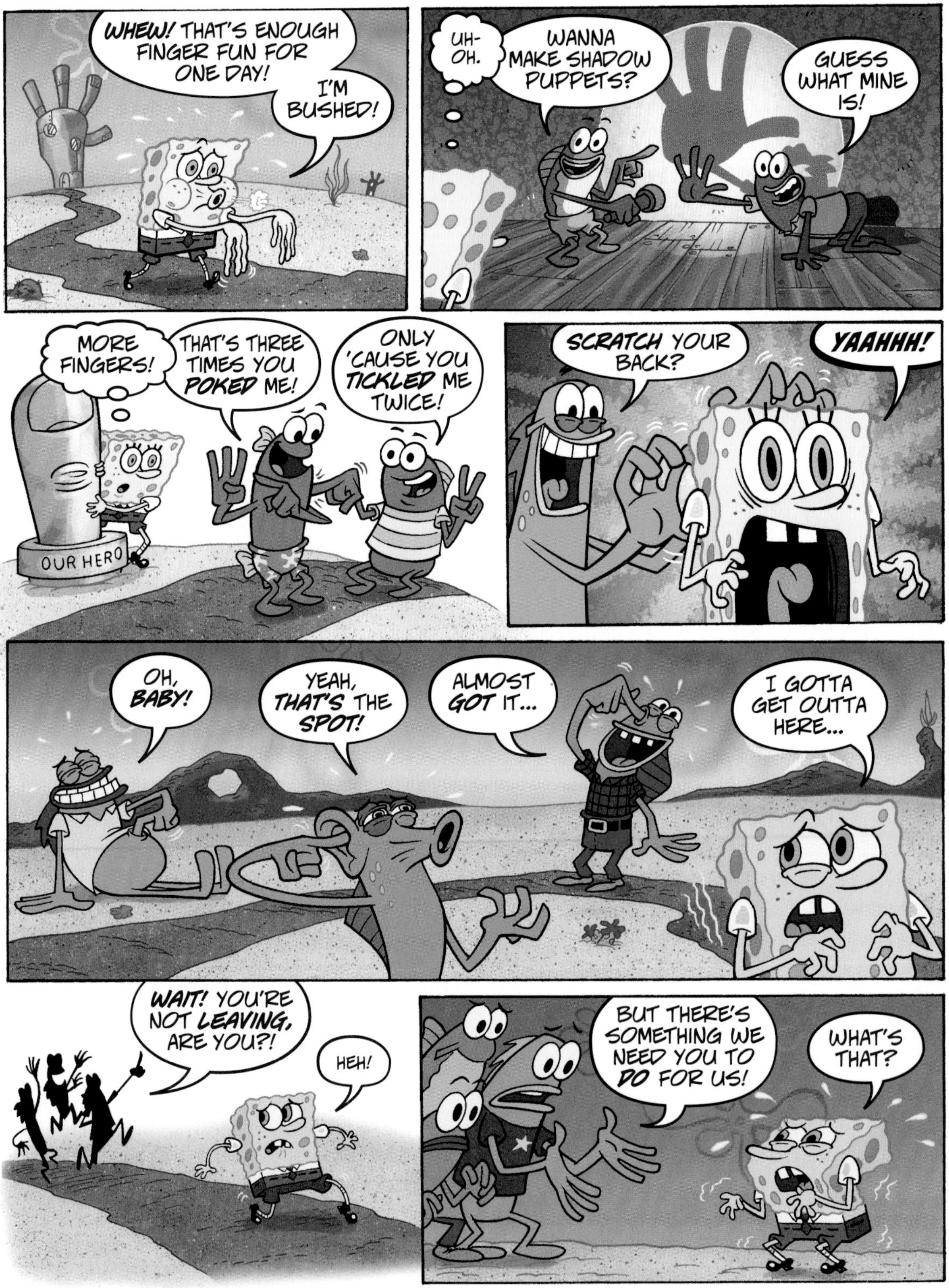
WHEW! THAT'S ENOUGH FINGER FUN FOR ONE DAY!
I'M BUSHED!
UH-OH.
WANNA MAKE SHADOW PUPPETS?
GUESS WHAT MINE IS!
MORE FINGERS!
OUR HERO
THAT'S THREE TIMES YOU POKED ME!
ONLY 'CAUSE YOU TICKLED ME TWICE!
SCRATCH YOUR BACK?
YAAHHH!
OH, BABY!
YEAH, THAT'S THE SPOT!
ALMOST GOT IT...
I GOTTA GET OUTTA HERE...
WAIT! YOU'RE NOT LEAVING, ARE YOU?!
HEH!
BUT THERE'S SOMETHING WE NEED YOU TO DO FOR US!
WHAT'S THAT?

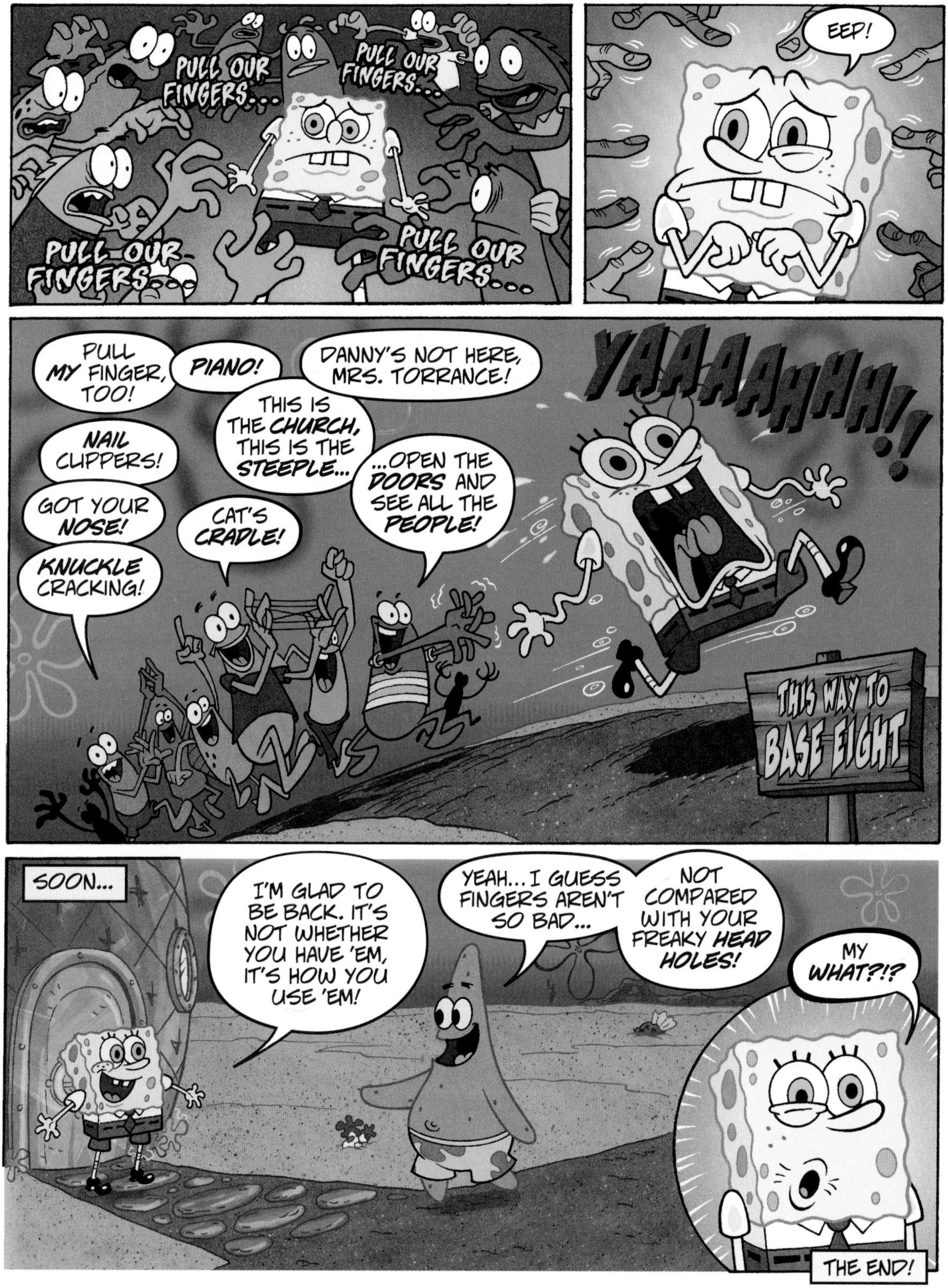
PULL OUR FINGERS...
PULL OUR FINGERS...
PULL OUR FINGERS...
PULL OUR FINGERS...
EEP!
PULL MY FINGER, TOO!
PIANO!
DANNY'S NOT HERE, MRS. TORRANCE!
YAAAAHHH!!
NAIL CLIPPERS!
THIS IS THE CHURCH, THIS IS THE STEEPLE...
...OPEN THE DOORS AND SEE ALL THE PEOPLE!
GOT YOUR NOSE!
CAT'S CRADLE!
KNUCKLE CRACKING!
THIS WAY TO BASE EIGHT
SOON...
I'M GLAD TO BE BACK. IT'S NOT WHETHER YOU HAVE 'EM, IT'S HOW YOU USE 'EM!
YEAH... I GUESS FINGERS AREN'T SO BAD...
NOT COMPARED WITH YOUR FREAKY HEAD HOLES!
MY WHAT?!?
THE END!

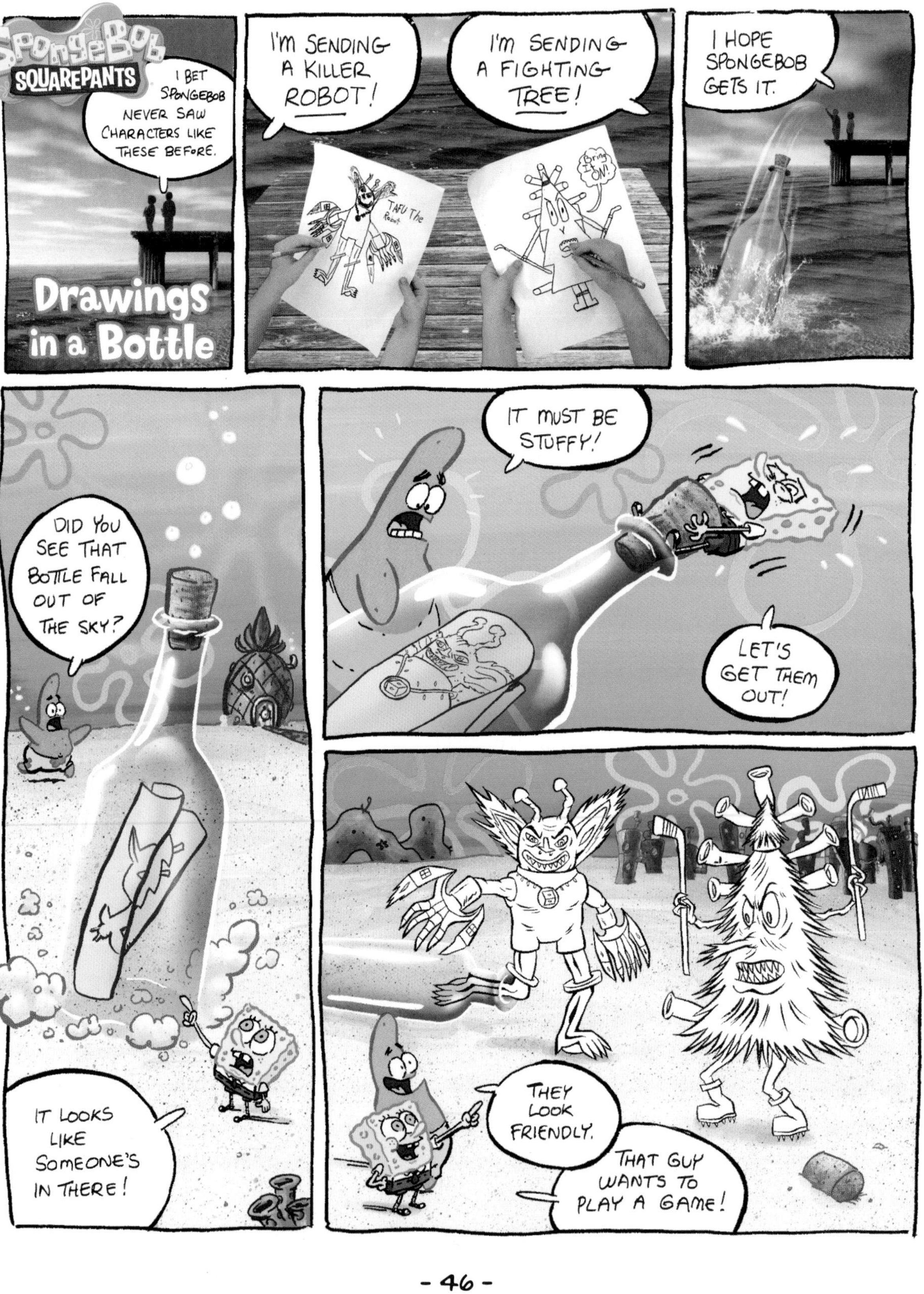
SpongeBob SquarePants
Drawings in a Bottle
I BET SPONGEBOB NEVER SAW CHARACTERS LIKE THESE BEFORE.
I'M SENDING A KILLER ROBOT!
I'M SENDING A FIGHTING TREE!
TAFU The Robot
Bring IT ON!
I HOPE SPONGEBOB GETS IT.
DID YOU SEE THAT BOTTLE FALL OUT OF THE SKY?
IT LOOKS LIKE SOMEONE'S IN THERE!
IT MUST BE STUFFY!
LET'S GET THEM OUT!
THEY LOOK FRIENDLY.
THAT GUY WANTS TO PLAY A GAME!

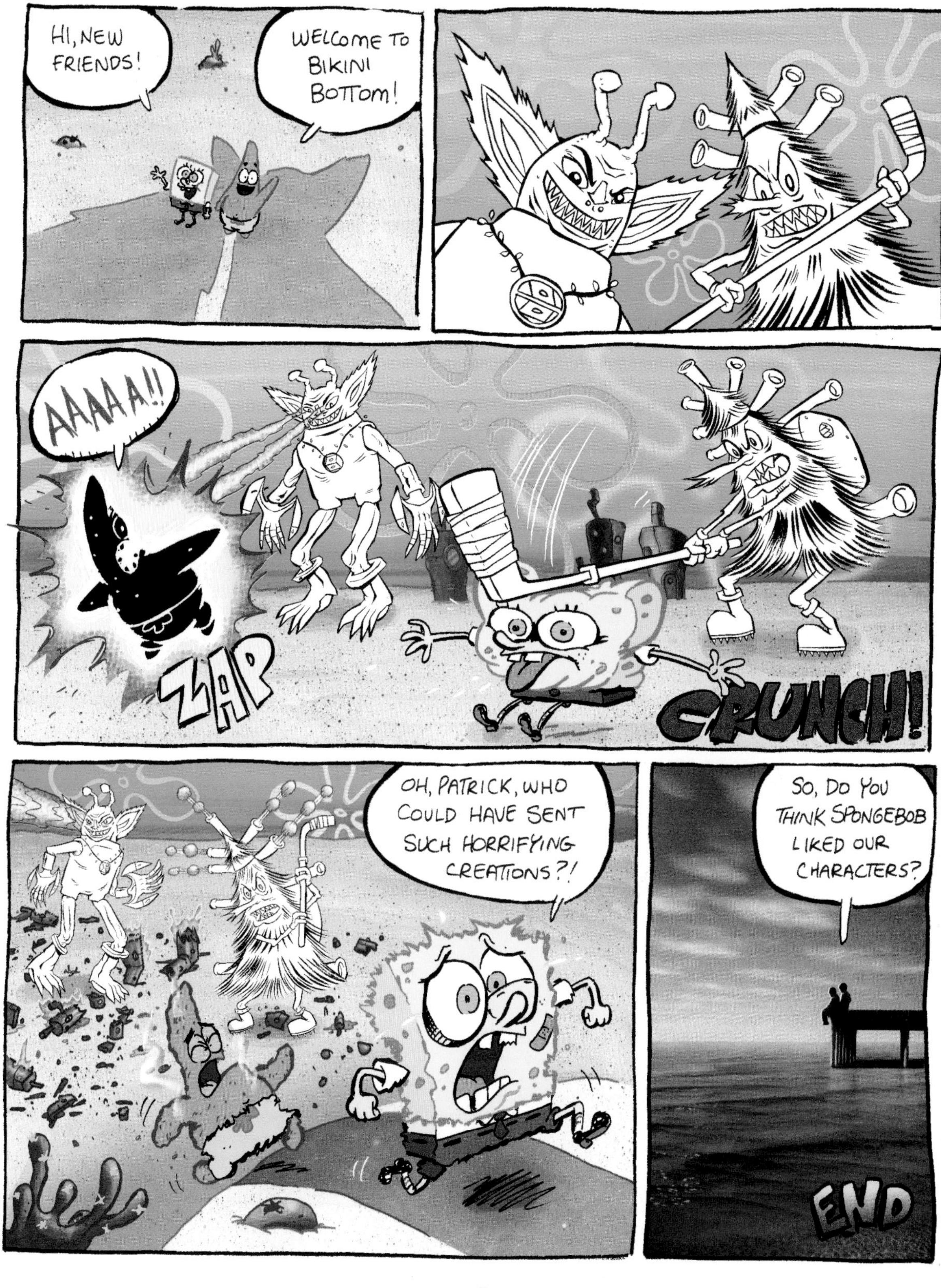
HI, NEW FRIENDS!
WELCOME TO BIKINI BOTTOM!
AAAAA!!
ZAP
CRUNCH!
OH, PATRICK, WHO COULD HAVE SENT SUCH HORRIFYING CREATIONS?!
SO, DO YOU THINK SPONGEBOB LIKED OUR CHARACTERS?
END

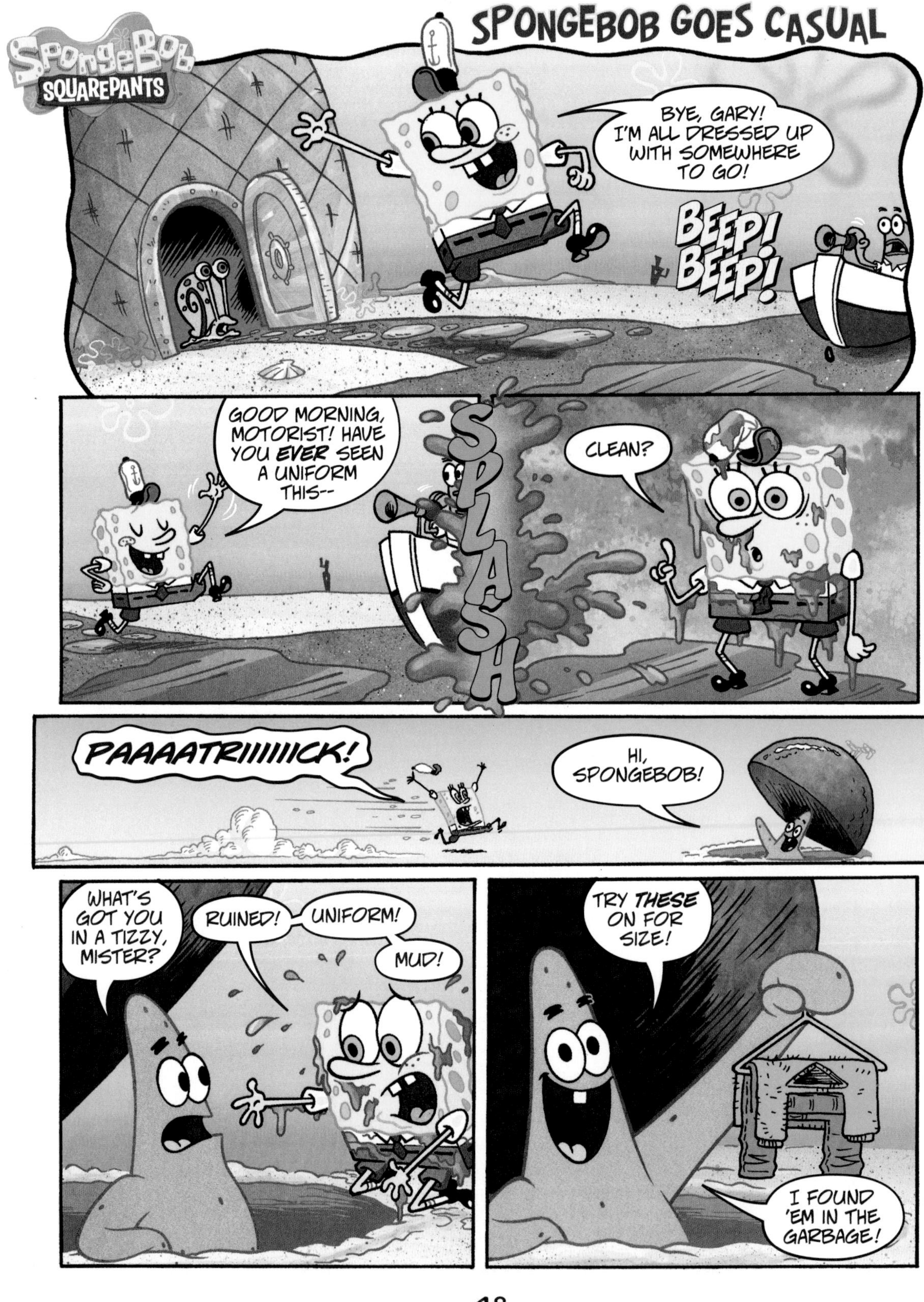
SPONGEBOB GOES CASUAL
SpongeBob SQUAREPANTS
BYE, GARY! I'M ALL DRESSED UP WITH SOMEWHERE TO GO!
BEEP! BEEP!
GOOD MORNING, MOTORIST! HAVE YOU EVER SEEN A UNIFORM THIS--
SPLASH
CLEAN?
PAAAATRIIIIIICK!
HI, SPONGEBOB!
WHAT'S GOT YOU IN A TIZZY, MISTER?
RUINED!
UNIFORM!
MUD!
TRY THESE ON FOR SIZE!
I FOUND 'EM IN THE GARBAGE!

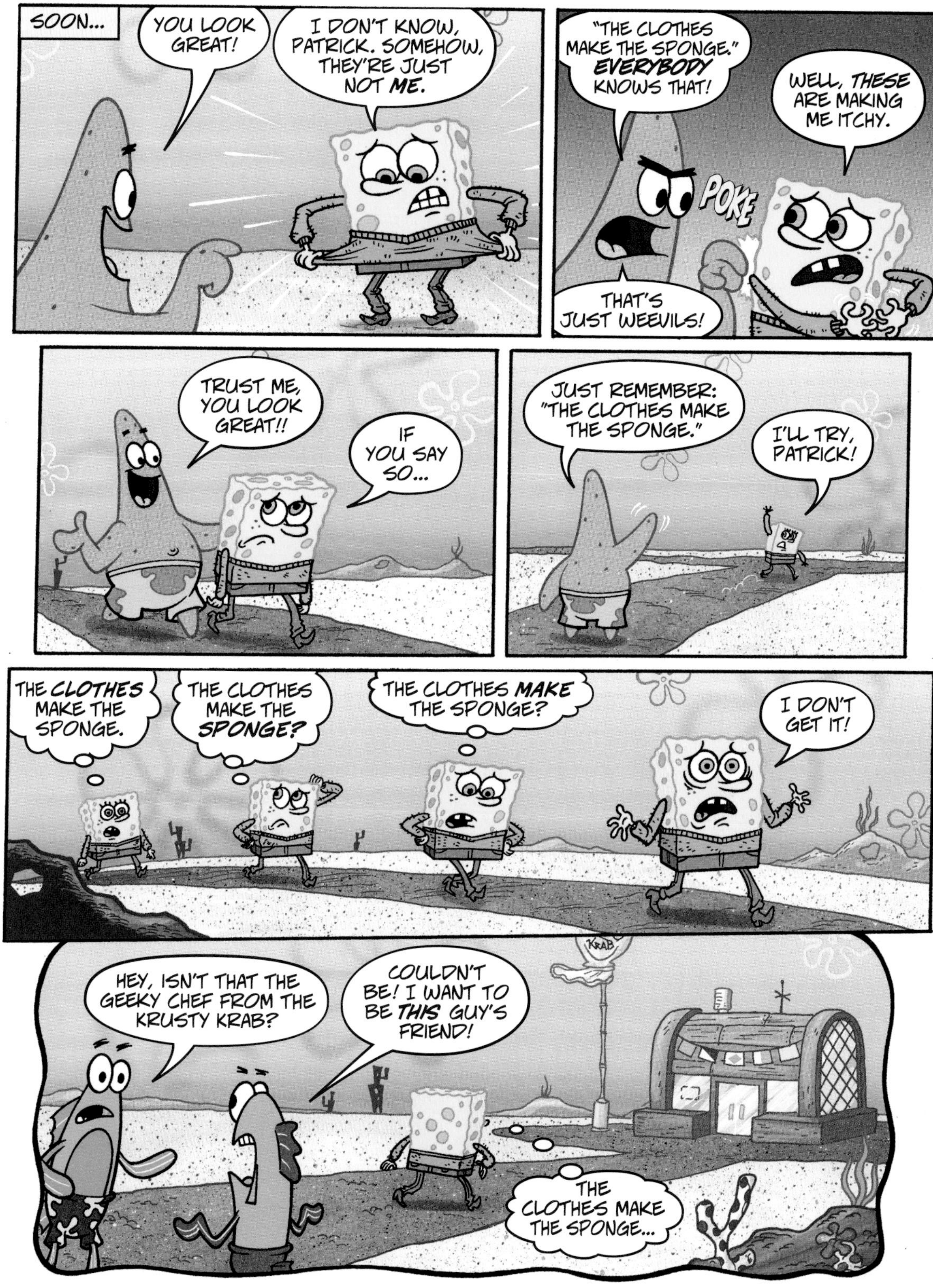

SOON...
YOU LOOK GREAT!
I DON'T KNOW, PATRICK. SOMEHOW, THEY'RE JUST NOT ME.
"THE CLOTHES MAKE THE SPONGE." EVERYBODY KNOWS THAT!
WELL, THESE ARE MAKING ME ITCHY.
POKE
THAT'S JUST WEEVILS!
TRUST ME, YOU LOOK GREAT!!
IF YOU SAY SO...
JUST REMEMBER: "THE CLOTHES MAKE THE SPONGE."
I'LL TRY, PATRICK!
THE CLOTHES MAKE THE SPONGE.
THE CLOTHES MAKE THE SPONGE?
THE CLOTHES MAKE THE SPONGE?
I DON'T GET IT!
HEY, ISN'T THAT THE GEEKY CHEF FROM THE KRUSTY KRAB?
COULDN'T BE! I WANT TO BE THIS GUY'S FRIEND!
KRAB
THE CLOTHES MAKE THE SPONGE...

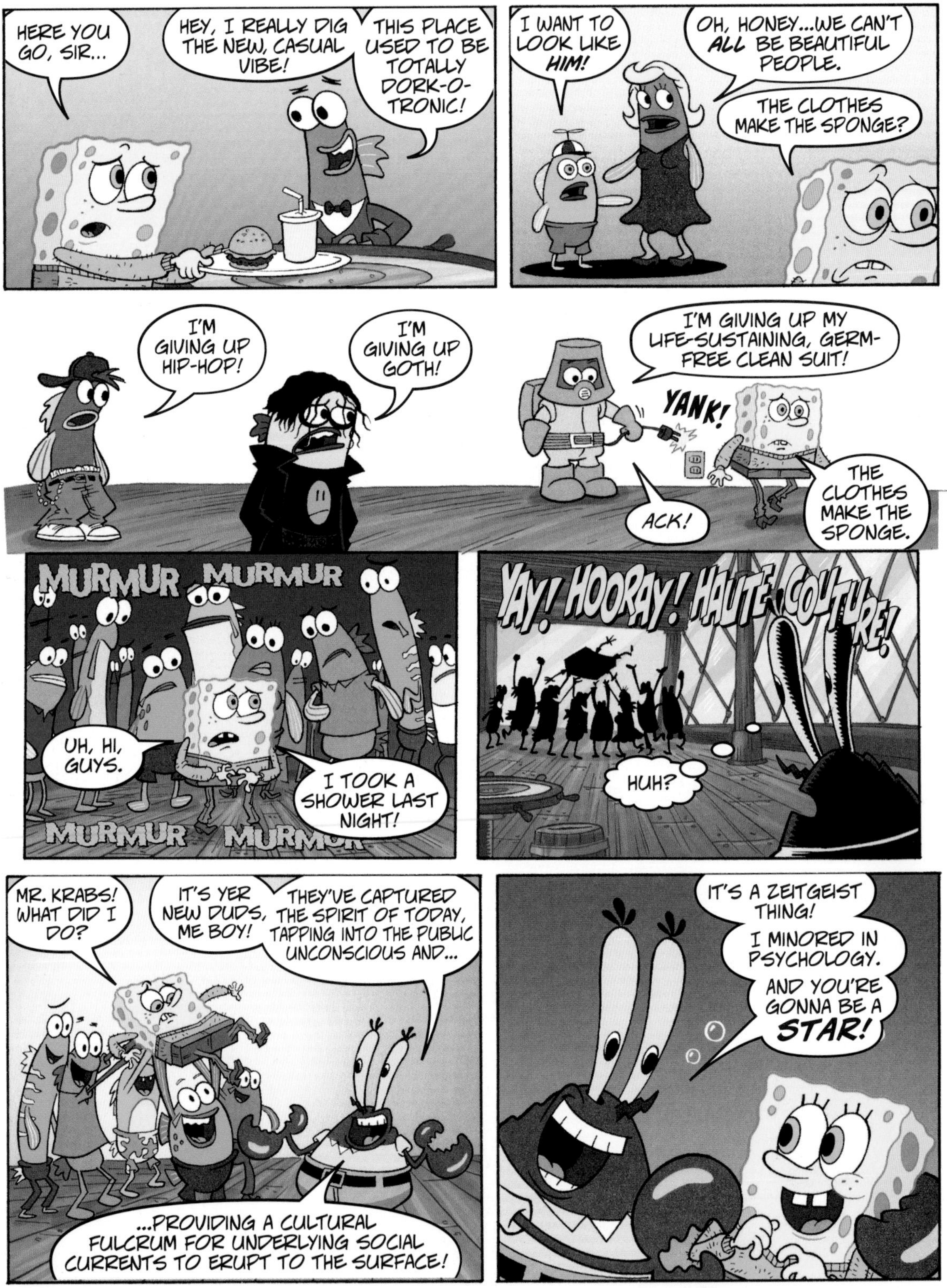
HERE YOU GO, SIR...
HEY, I REALLY DIG THE NEW, CASUAL VIBE!
THIS PLACE USED TO BE TOTALLY DORK-O-TRONIC!
I WANT TO LOOK LIKE HIM!
OH, HONEY...WE CAN'T ALL BE BEAUTIFUL PEOPLE.
THE CLOTHES MAKE THE SPONGE?
I'M GIVING UP HIP-HOP!
I'M GIVING UP GOTH!
I'M GIVING UP MY LIFE-SUSTAINING, GERM-FREE CLEAN SUIT!
YANK!
ACK!
THE CLOTHES MAKE THE SPONGE.
MURMUR MURMUR
UH, HI, GUYS.
I TOOK A SHOWER LAST NIGHT!
MURMUR MURMUR
YAY! HOORAY! HAUTE COUTURE!
HUH?
MR. KRABS! WHAT DID I DO?
IT'S YER NEW DUDS, ME BOY!
THEY'VE CAPTURED THE SPIRIT OF TODAY, TAPPING INTO THE PUBLIC UNCONSCIOUS AND...
...PROVIDING A CULTURAL FULCRUM FOR UNDERLYING SOCIAL CURRENTS TO ERUPT TO THE SURFACE!
IT'S A ZEITGEIST THING!
I MINORED IN PSYCHOLOGY.
AND YOU'RE GONNA BE A STAR!

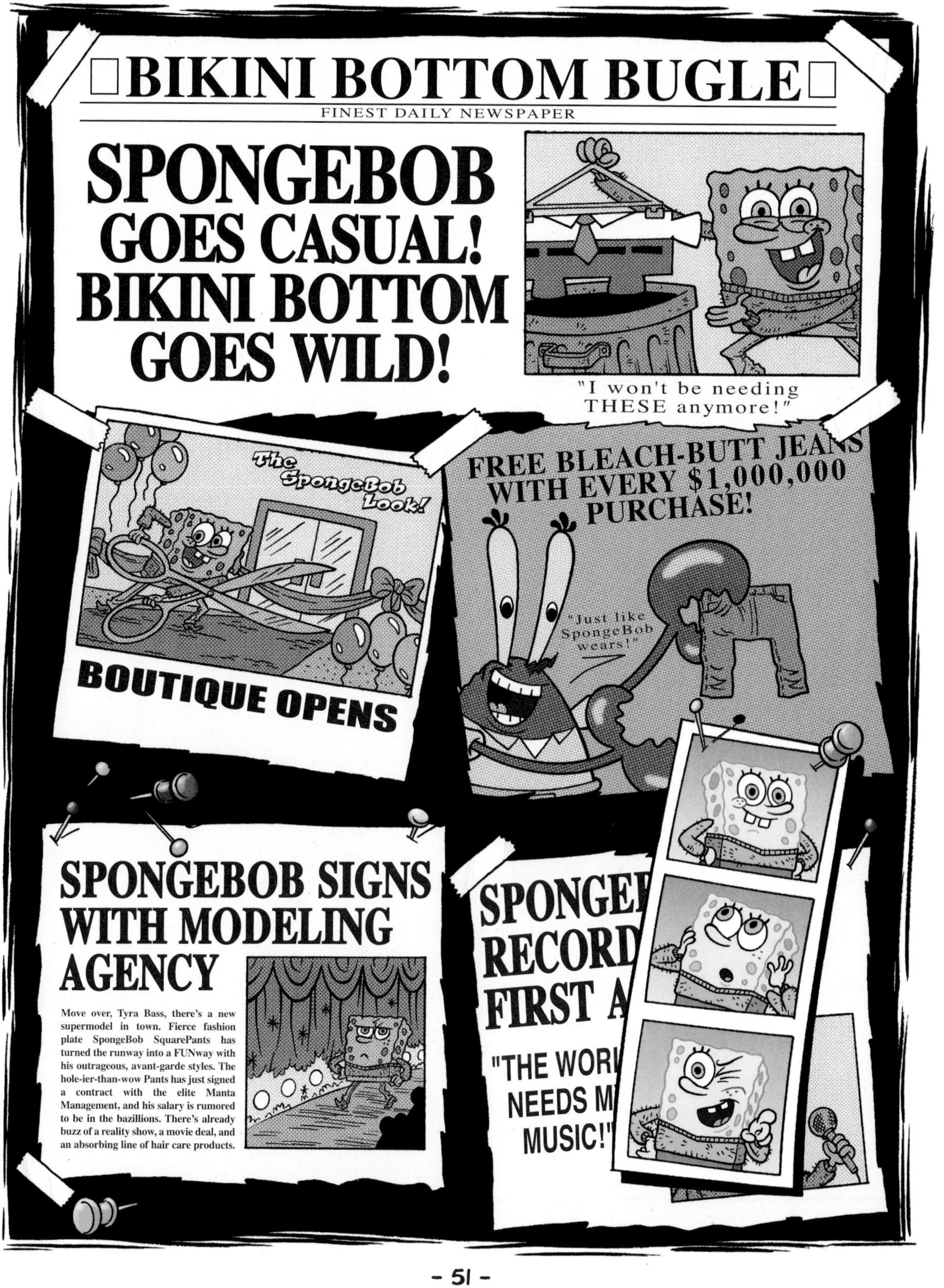
BIKINI BOTTOM BUGLE
FINEST DAILY NEWSPAPER
SPONGEBOB GOES CASUAL! BIKINI BOTTOM GOES WILD!
"I won't be needing THESE anymore!"
The SpongeBob Look!
BOUTIQUE OPENS
FREE BLEACH-BUTT JEANS WITH EVERY $1,000,000 PURCHASE!
"Just like SpongeBob wears!"
SPONGEBOB SIGNS WITH MODELING AGENCY
Move over, Tyra Bass, there's a new supermodel in town. Fierce fashion plate SpongeBob SquarePants has turned the runway into a FUNway with his outrageous, avant-garde styles. The hole-ier-than-wow Pants has just signed a contract with the elite Manta Management, and his salary is rumored to be in the bazillions. There's already buzz of a reality show, a movie deal, and an absorbing line of hair care products.
SPONGE
RECORD
FIRST A
"THE WOR
NEEDS M
MUSIC!"

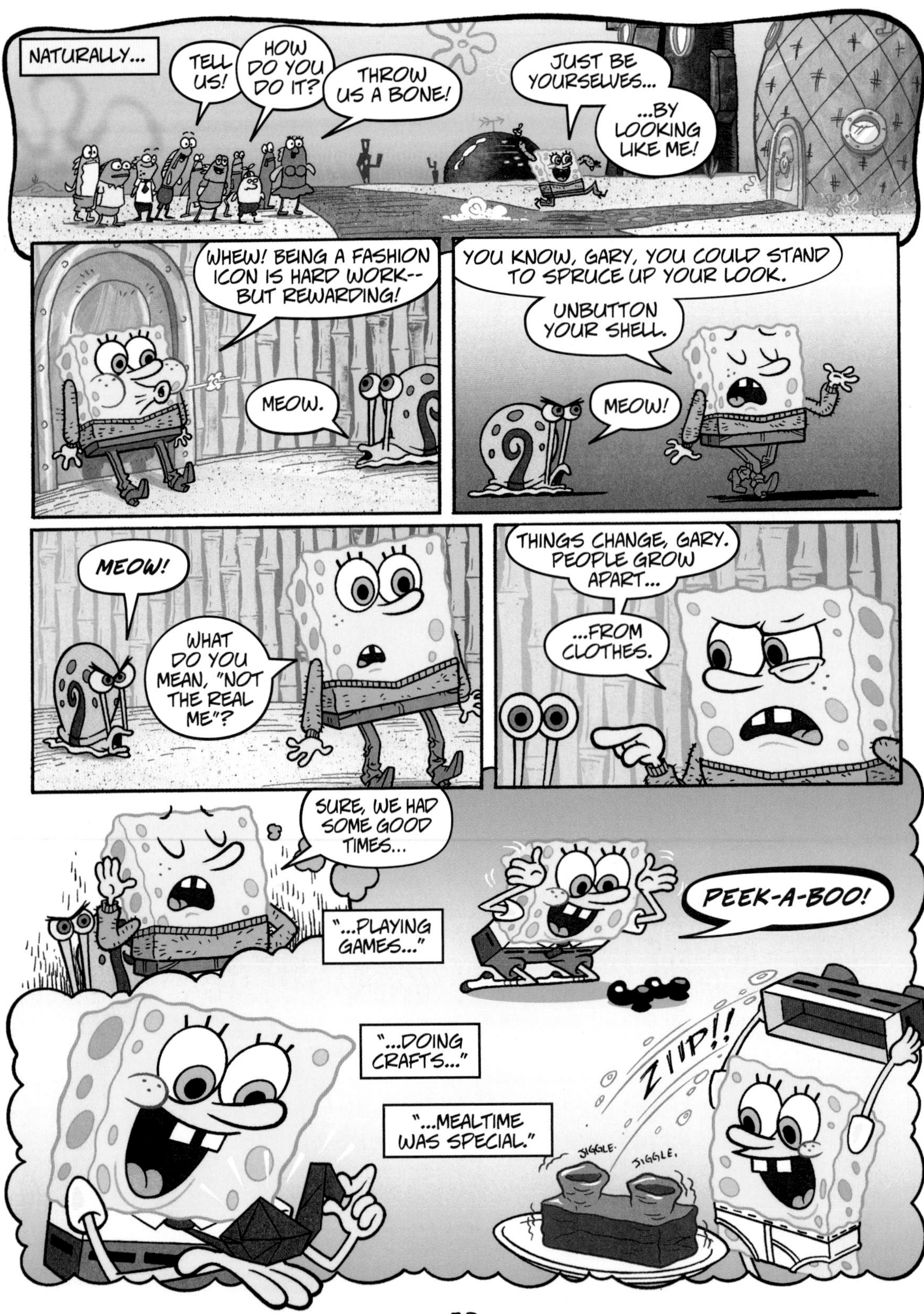
NATURALLY...
TELL US!
HOW DO YOU DO IT?
THROW US A BONE!
JUST BE YOURSELVES...
...BY LOOKING LIKE ME!
WHEW! BEING A FASHION ICON IS HARD WORK-- BUT REWARDING!
MEOW.
YOU KNOW, GARY, YOU COULD STAND TO SPRUCE UP YOUR LOOK.
UNBUTTON YOUR SHELL.
MEOW!
MEOW!
WHAT DO YOU MEAN, "NOT THE REAL ME"?
THINGS CHANGE, GARY. PEOPLE GROW APART...
...FROM CLOTHES.
SURE, WE HAD SOME GOOD TIMES...
"...PLAYING GAMES..."
PEEK-A-BOO!
"...DOING CRAFTS..."
"...MEALTIME WAS SPECIAL."
ZIIIP!!
JIGGLE.
JIGGLE.

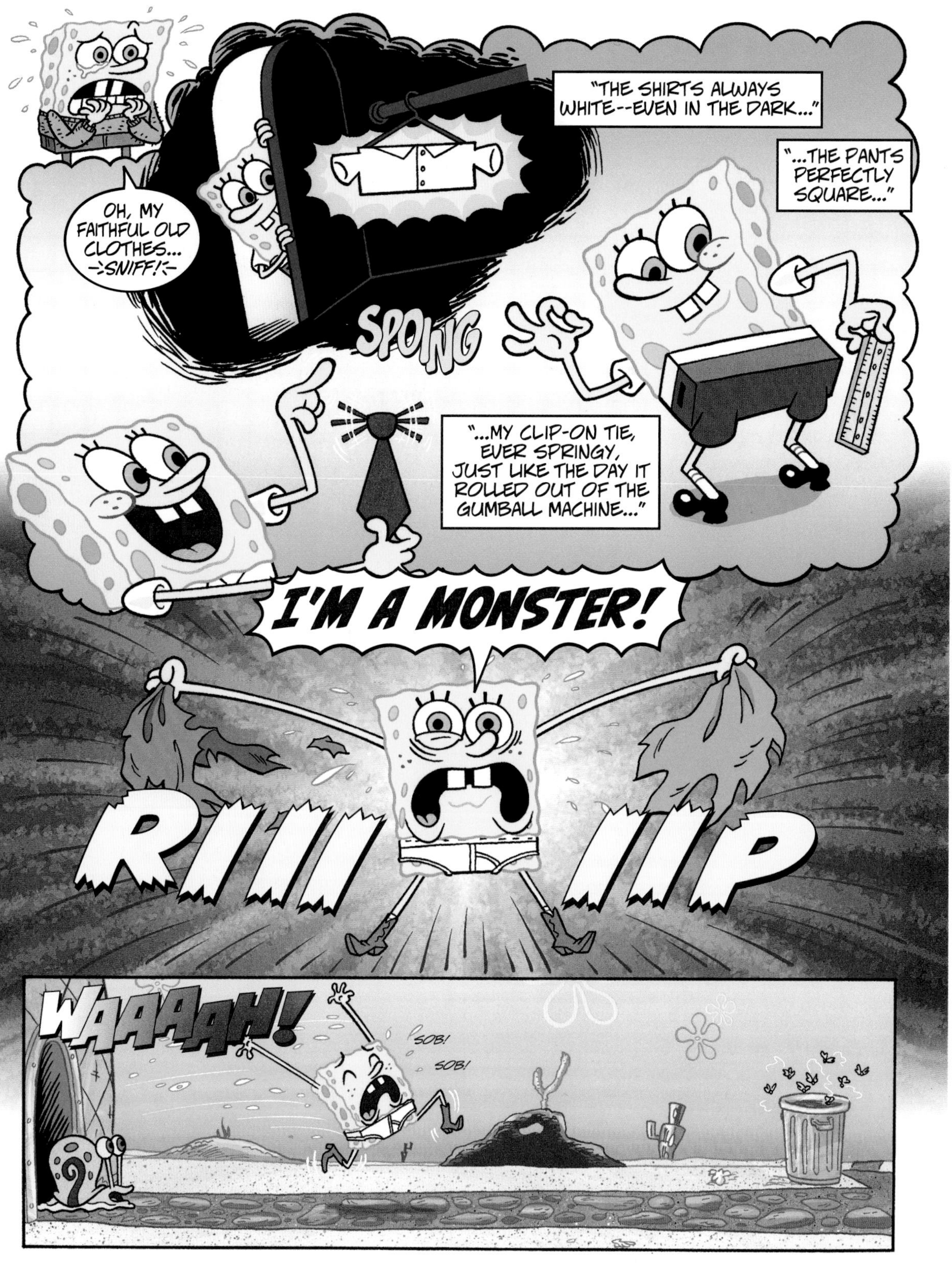
"THE SHIRTS ALWAYS WHITE--EVEN IN THE DARK..."
OH, MY FAITHFUL OLD CLOTHES... -SNIFF!-
"...THE PANTS PERFECTLY SQUARE..."
SPOING
"...MY CLIP-ON TIE, EVER SPRINGY, JUST LIKE THE DAY IT ROLLED OUT OF THE GUMBALL MACHINE..."
I'M A MONSTER!
RIII IIP
WAAAAH!
SOB!
SOB!

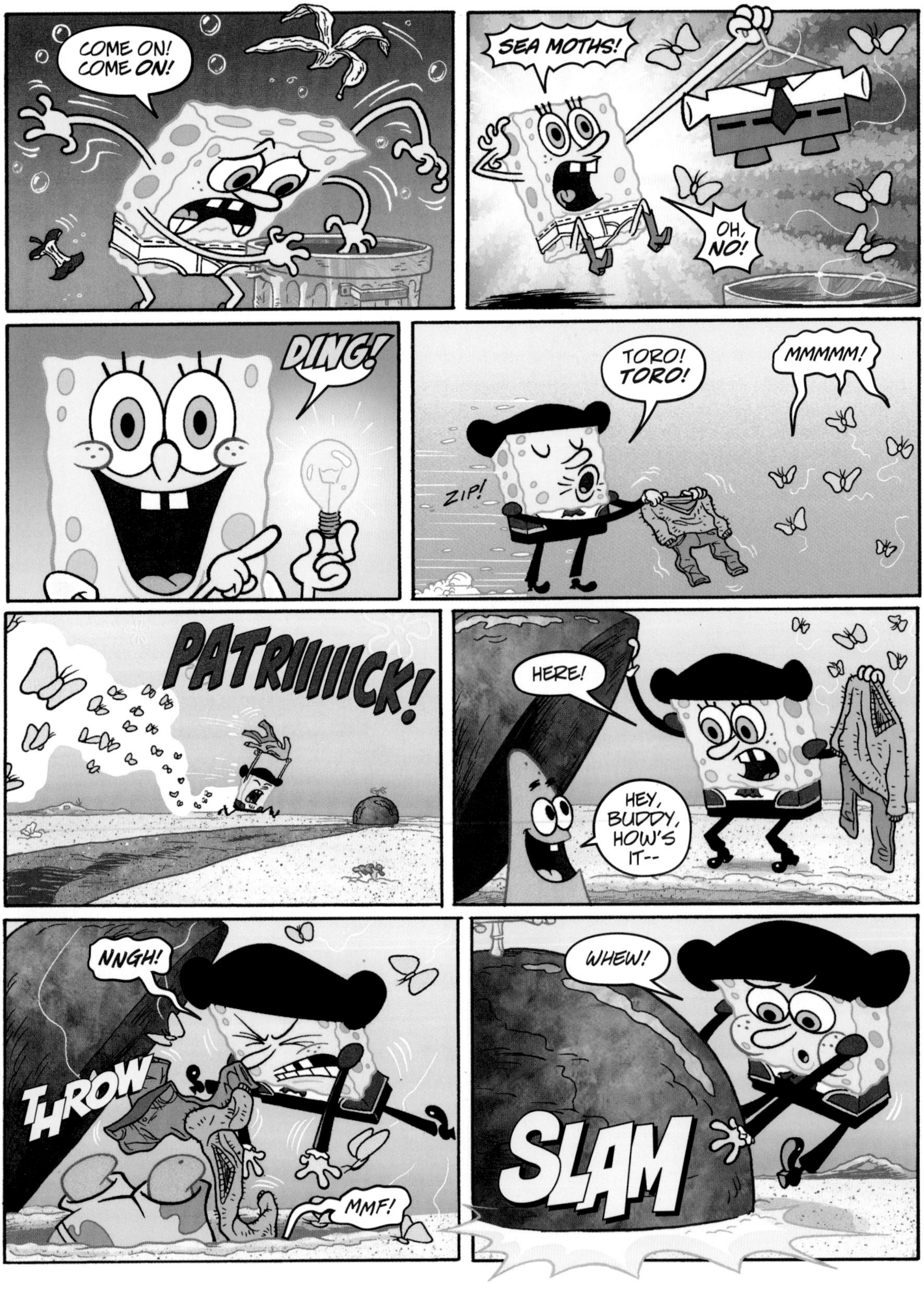
COME ON!
COME ON!
SEA MOTHS!
OH, NO!
DING!
TORO! TORO!
MMMMM!
ZIP!
PATRIIIIICK!
HERE!
HEY, BUDDY, HOW'S IT--
NNGH!
THROW
MMF!
WHEW!
SLAM

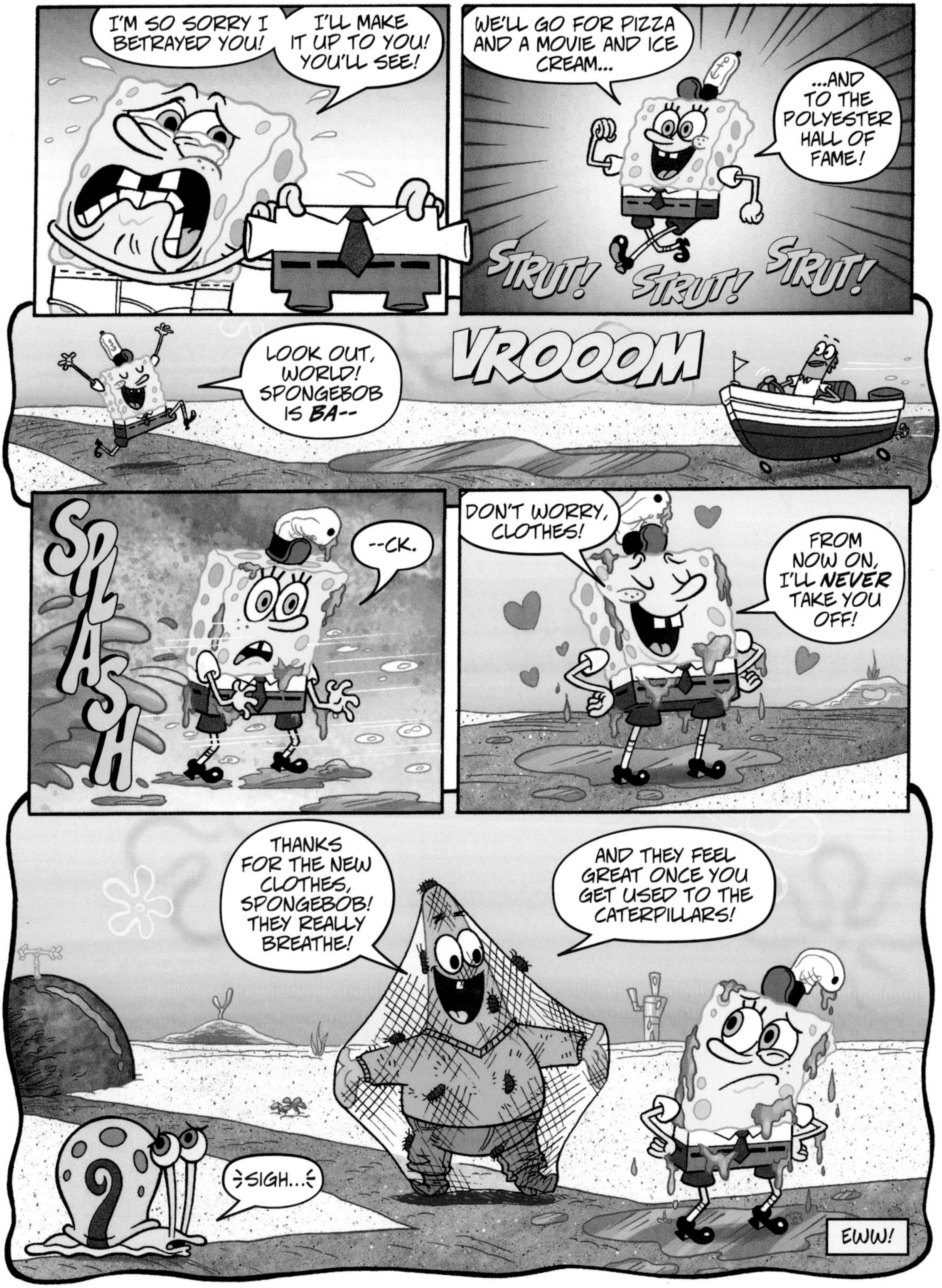
I'M SO SORRY I BETRAYED YOU!
I'LL MAKE IT UP TO YOU! YOU'LL SEE!
WE'LL GO FOR PIZZA AND A MOVIE AND ICE CREAM...
...AND TO THE POLYESTER HALL OF FAME!
STRUT! STRUT! STRUT!
LOOK OUT, WORLD! SPONGEBOB IS **BA--**
VROOOM
SPLASH
--CK.
DON'T WORRY, CLOTHES!
FROM NOW ON, I'LL **NEVER** TAKE YOU OFF!
THANKS FOR THE NEW CLOTHES, SPONGEBOB! THEY REALLY BREATHE!
AND THEY FEEL GREAT ONCE YOU GET USED TO THE CATERPILLARS!
SIGH...
EWW!

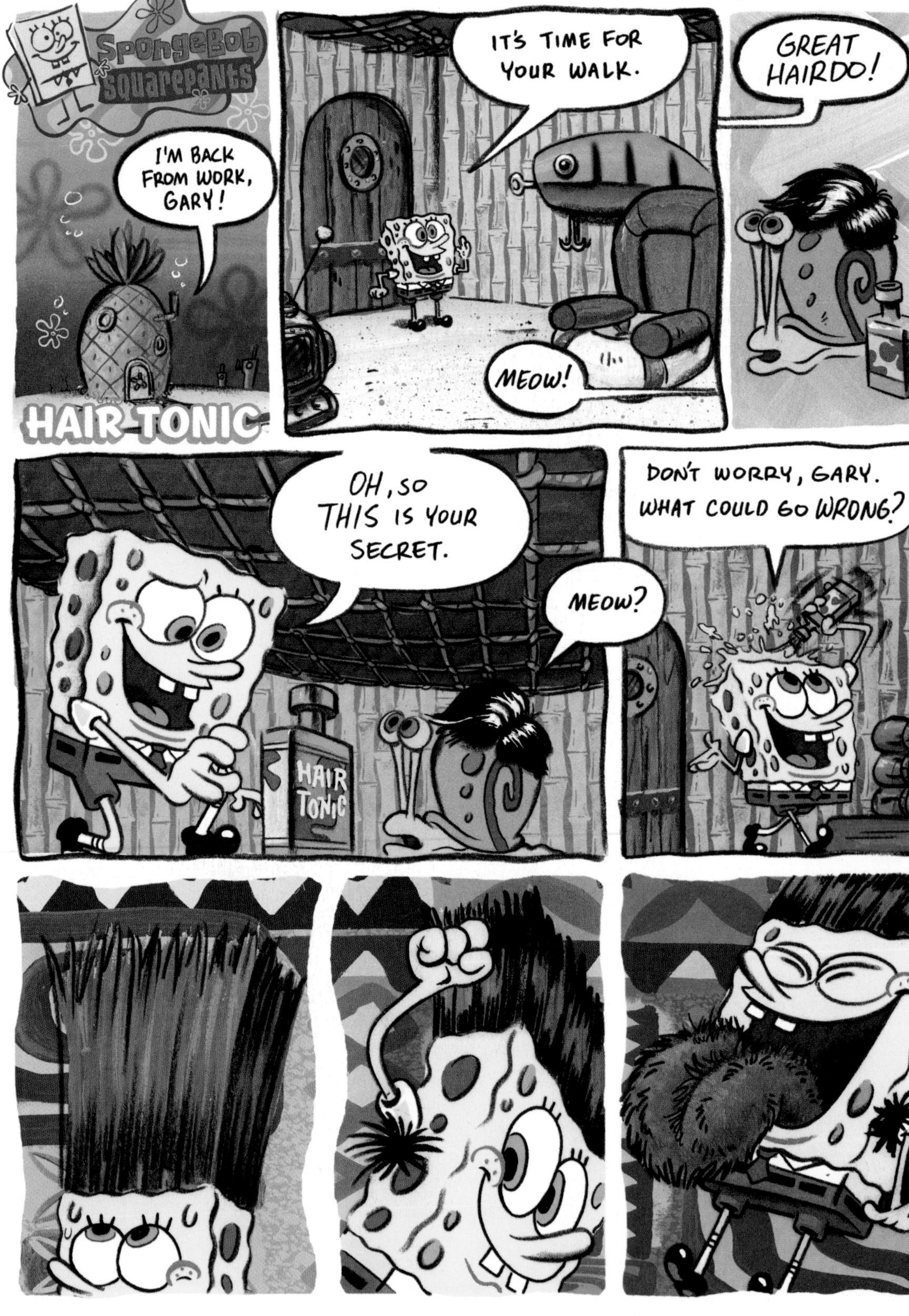
SpongeBob SquarePants
HAIR TONIC
I'M BACK FROM WORK, GARY!
IT'S TIME FOR YOUR WALK.
MEOW!
GREAT HAIRDO!
OH, SO THIS IS YOUR SECRET.
MEOW?
HAIR TONIC
DON'T WORRY, GARY. WHAT COULD GO WRONG?

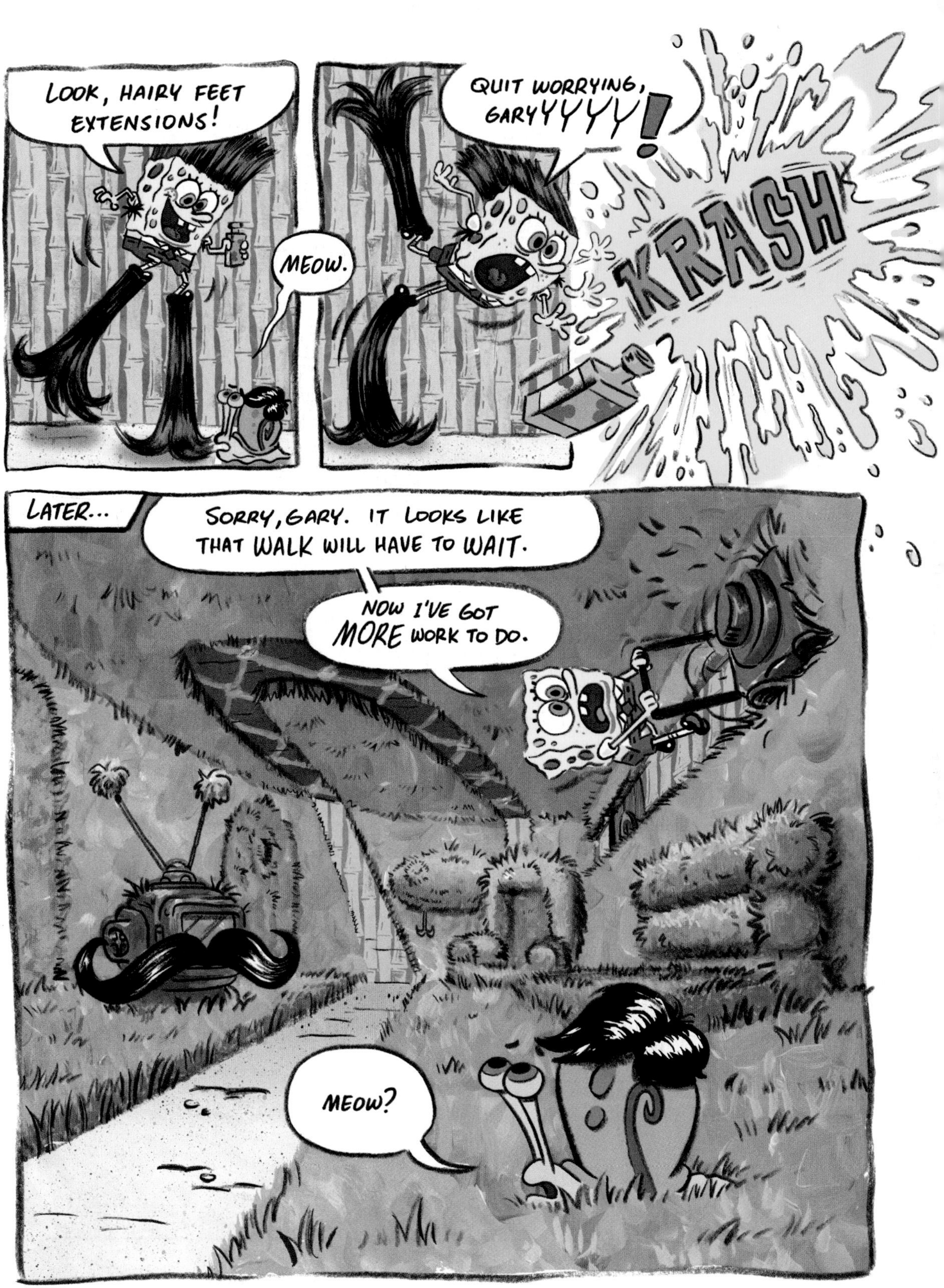
LOOK, HAIRY FEET EXTENSIONS!
MEOW.
QUIT WORRYING, GARYYYYY!
KRASH
LATER...
SORRY, GARY. IT LOOKS LIKE THAT WALK WILL HAVE TO WAIT.
NOW I'VE GOT MORE WORK TO DO.
MEOW?

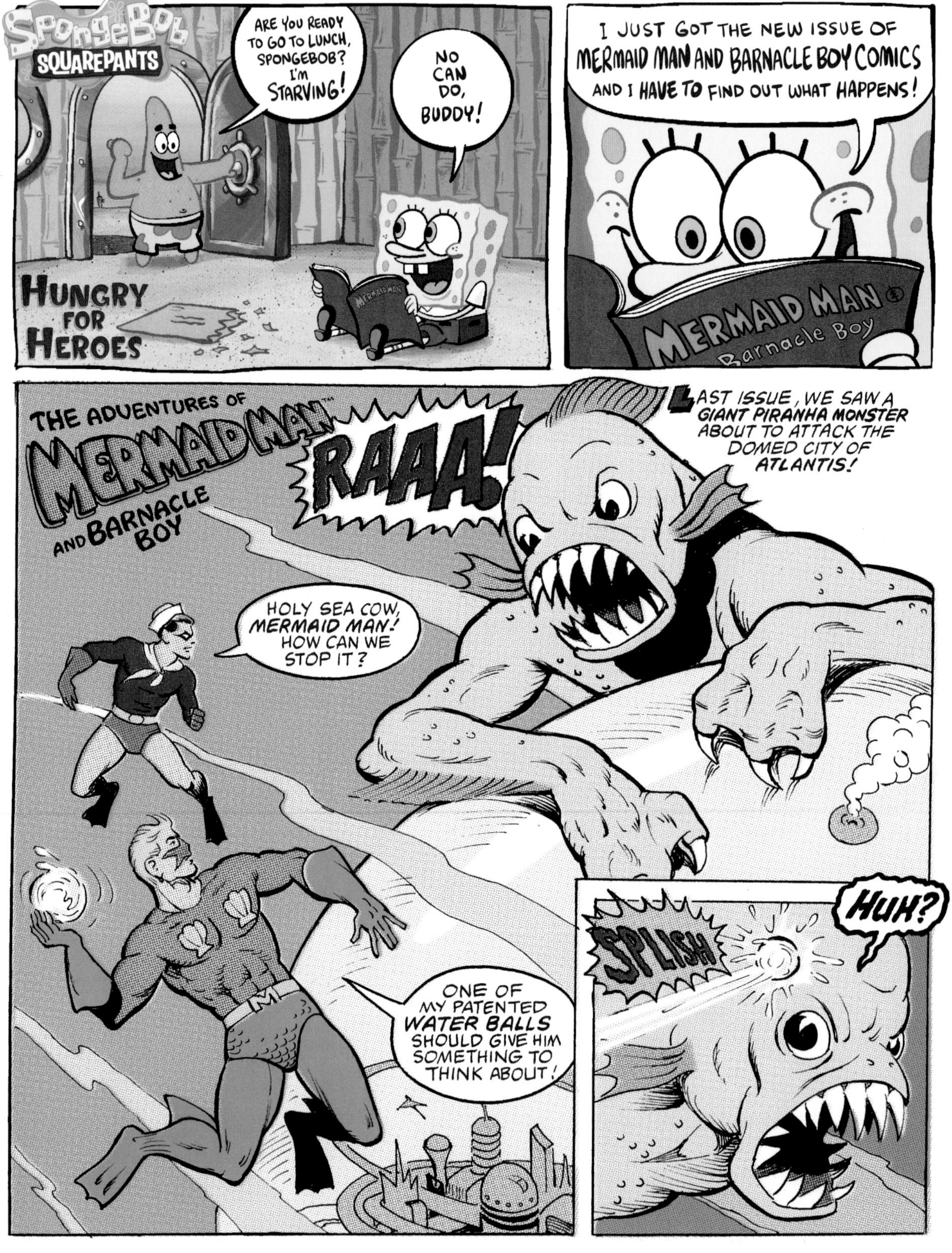
SpongeBob SQUAREPANTS
HUNGRY FOR HEROES
ARE YOU READY TO GO TO LUNCH, SPONGEBOB? I'M STARVING!
NO CAN DO, BUDDY!
MERMAID MAN
I JUST GOT THE NEW ISSUE OF MERMAID MAN AND BARNACLE BOY COMICS AND I HAVE TO FIND OUT WHAT HAPPENS!
MERMAID MAN
Barnacle Boy
THE ADVENTURES OF MERMAID MAN™ AND BARNACLE BOY
RAAA!
LAST ISSUE, WE SAW A GIANT PIRANHA MONSTER ABOUT TO ATTACK THE DOMED CITY OF ATLANTIS!
HOLY SEA COW, MERMAID MAN! HOW CAN WE STOP IT?
ONE OF MY PATENTED WATER BALLS SHOULD GIVE HIM SOMETHING TO THINK ABOUT!
SPLISH
HUH?

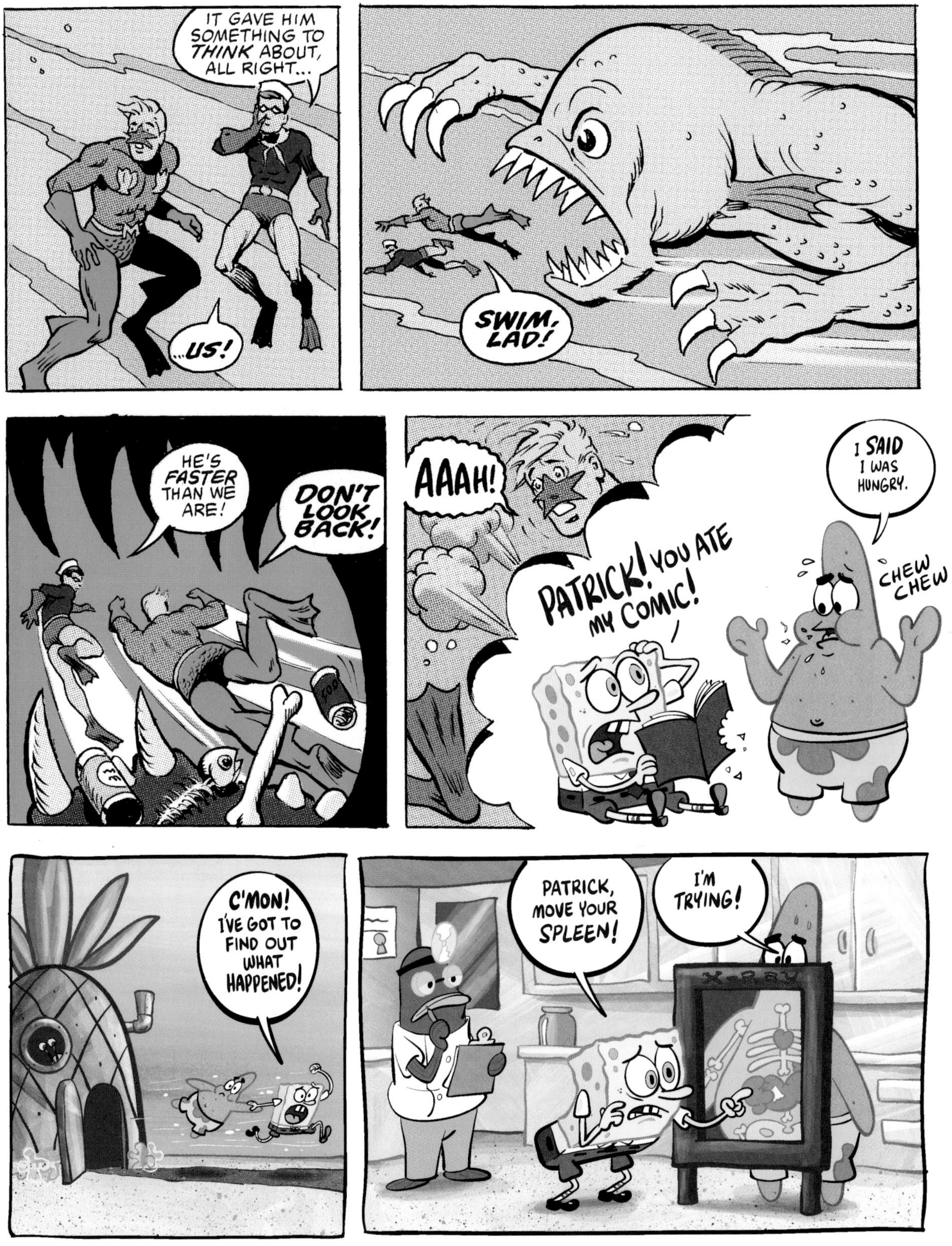
IT GAVE HIM SOMETHING TO THINK ABOUT, ALL RIGHT...
...US!
SWIM, LAD!
HE'S FASTER THAN WE ARE!
DON'T LOOK BACK!
AAAH!
PATRICK! YOU ATE MY COMIC!
I SAID I WAS HUNGRY.
CHEW CHEW
C'MON! I'VE GOT TO FIND OUT WHAT HAPPENED!
PATRICK, MOVE YOUR SPLEEN!
I'M TRYING!
X-RAY

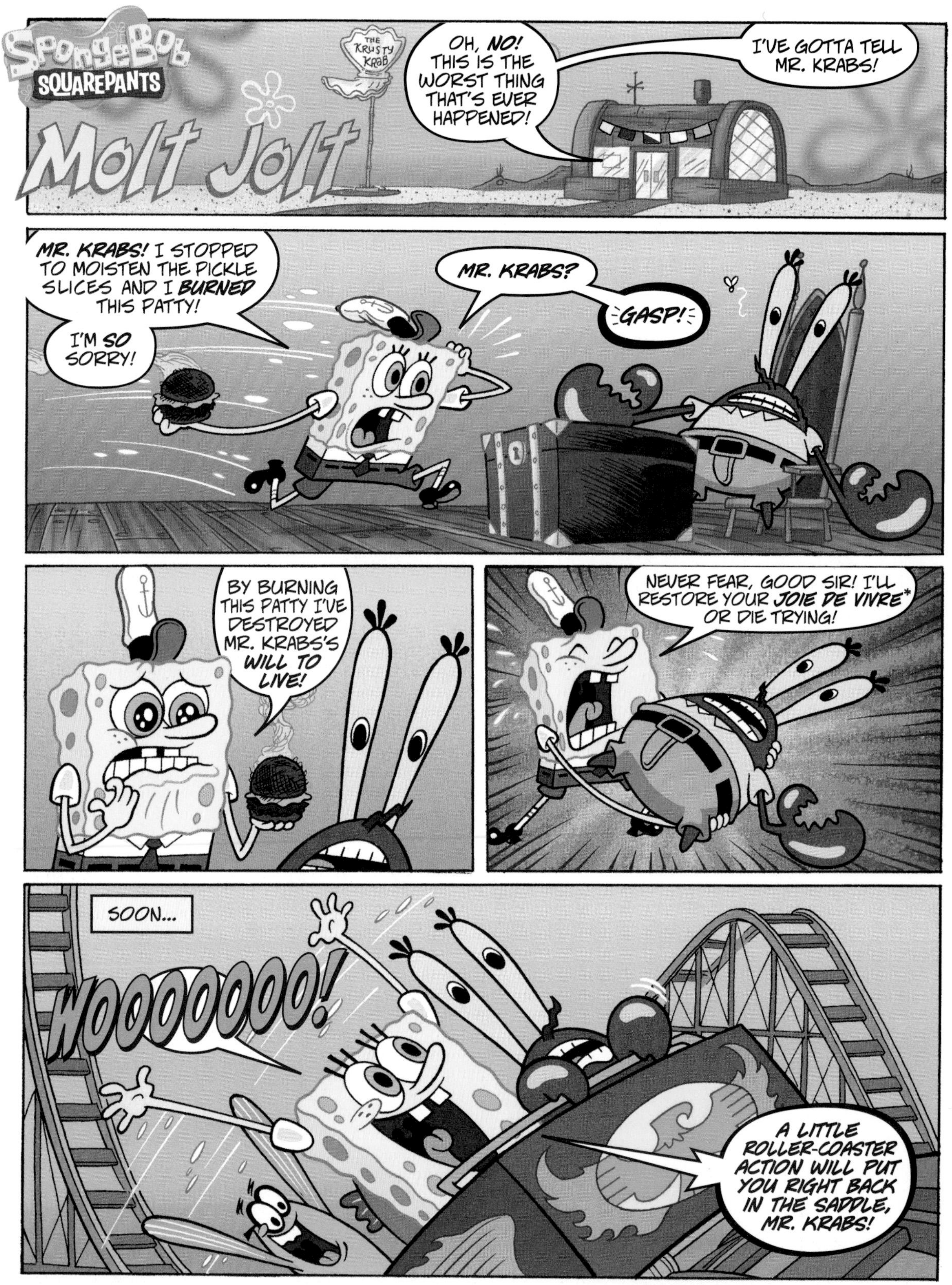
SpongeBob SquarePants
Molt Jolt
THE KRUSTY KRAB
OH, NO! THIS IS THE WORST THING THAT'S EVER HAPPENED!
I'VE GOTTA TELL MR. KRABS!
MR. KRABS! I STOPPED TO MOISTEN THE PICKLE SLICES AND I BURNED THIS PATTY!
I'M SO SORRY!
MR. KRABS?
GASP!
BY BURNING THIS PATTY I'VE DESTROYED MR. KRABS'S WILL TO LIVE!
NEVER FEAR, GOOD SIR! I'LL RESTORE YOUR JOIE DE VIVRE* OR DIE TRYING!
SOON...
WOOOOOOO!
A LITTLE ROLLER-COASTER ACTION WILL PUT YOU RIGHT BACK IN THE SADDLE, MR. KRABS!

*JOIE DE VIVRE MEANS "ENJOYMENT OF LIFE."

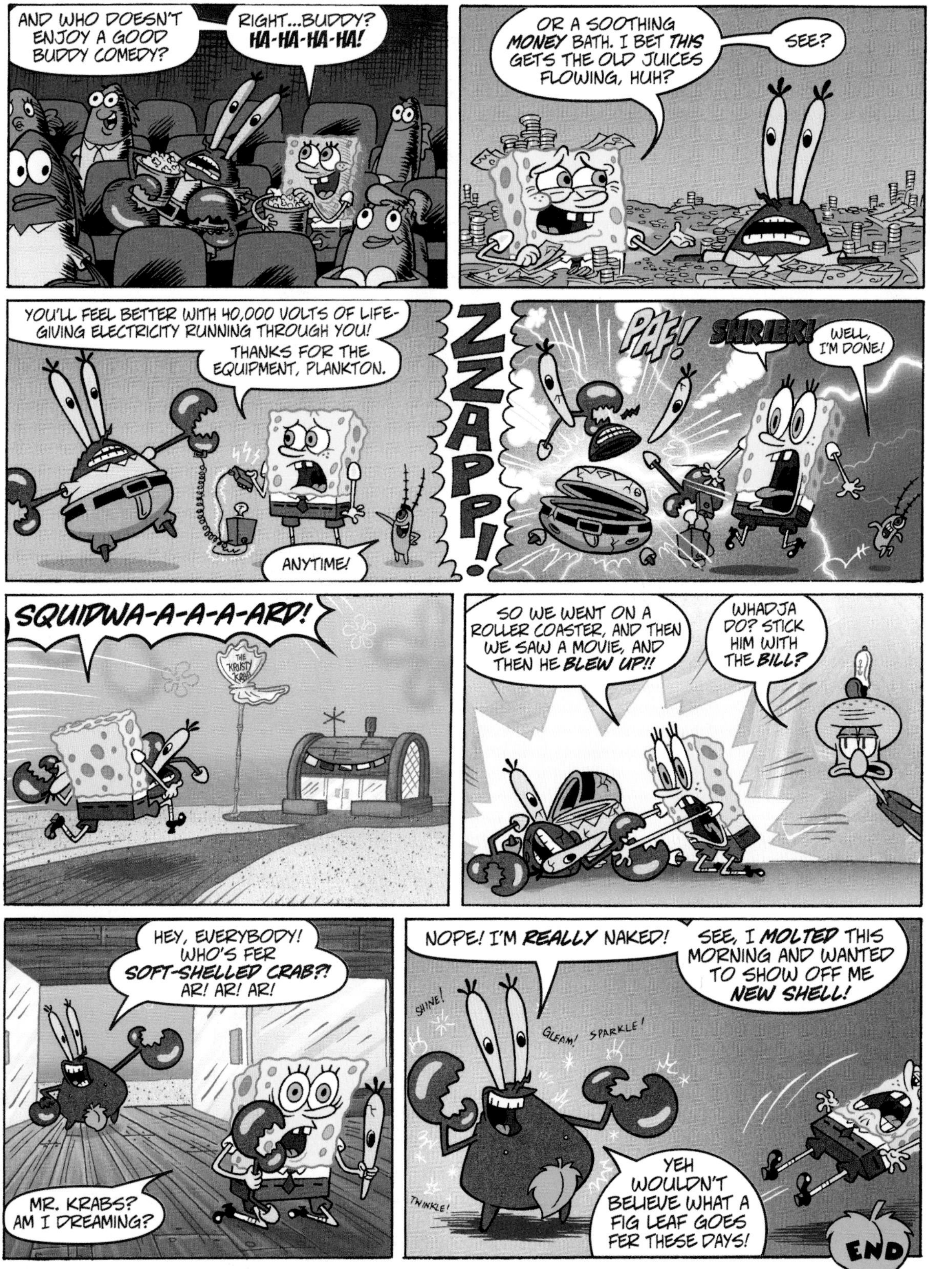
AND WHO DOESN'T ENJOY A GOOD BUDDY COMEDY?
RIGHT...BUDDY? HA-HA-HA-HA!
OR A SOOTHING MONEY BATH. I BET THIS GETS THE OLD JUICES FLOWING, HUH?
SEE?
YOU'LL FEEL BETTER WITH 40,000 VOLTS OF LIFE-GIVING ELECTRICITY RUNNING THROUGH YOU!
THANKS FOR THE EQUIPMENT, PLANKTON.
ANYTIME!
ZZAPP!
PAF!
SHRIEK!
WELL, I'M DONE!
SQUIDWA-A-A-ARD!
THE KRUSTY KRAB
SO WE WENT ON A ROLLER COASTER, AND THEN WE SAW A MOVIE, AND THEN HE BLEW UP!!
WHADJA DO? STICK HIM WITH THE BILL?
HEY, EVERYBODY! WHO'S FER SOFT-SHELLED CRAB?! AR! AR! AR!
MR. KRABS? AM I DREAMING?
NOPE! I'M REALLY NAKED!
SEE, I MOLTED THIS MORNING AND WANTED TO SHOW OFF ME NEW SHELL!
SHINE!
GLEAM!
SPARKLE!
TWINKLE!
YEH WOULDN'T BELIEVE WHAT A FIG LEAF GOES FER THESE DAYS!
END

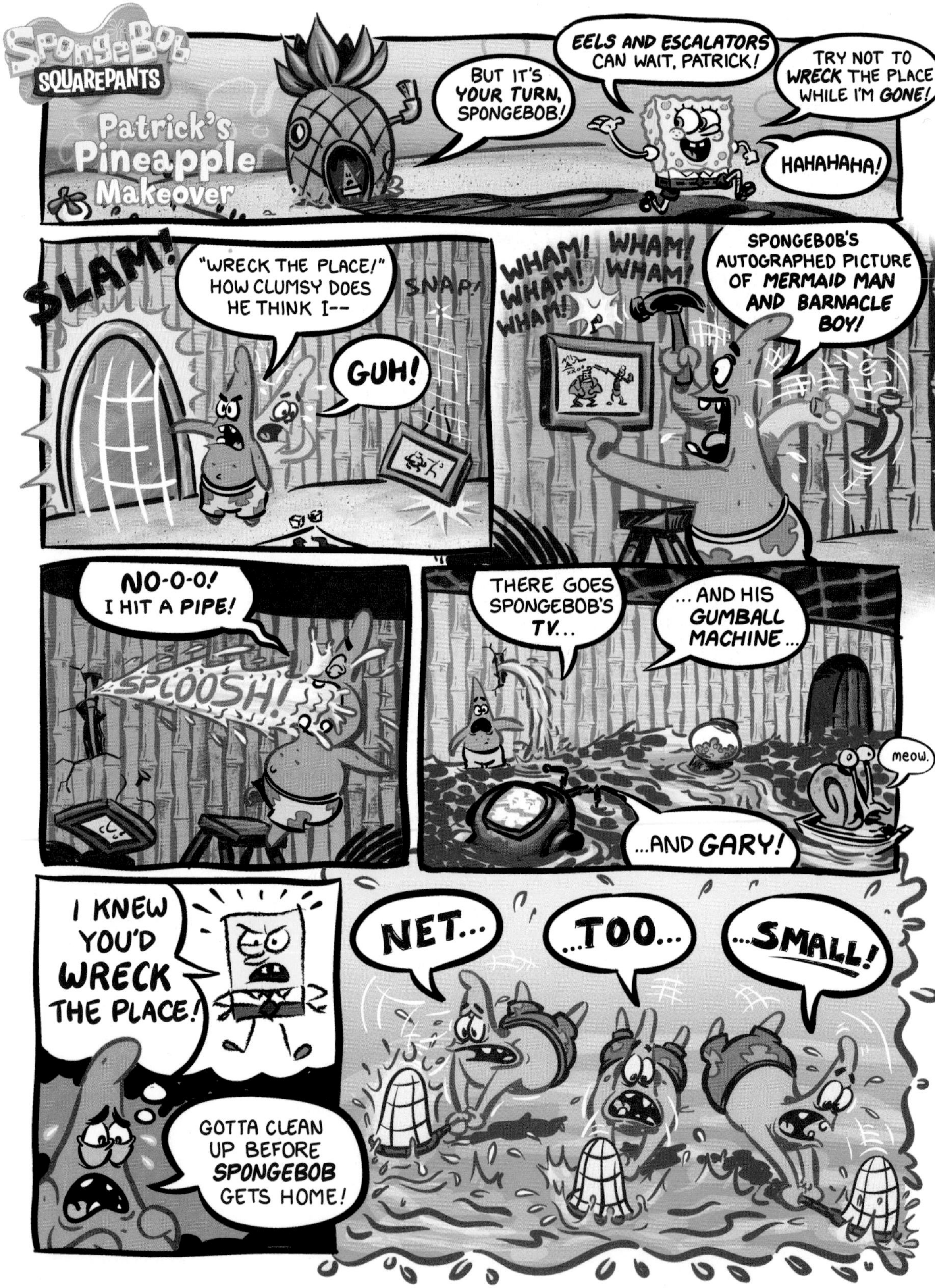
SpongeBob SQUAREPANTS
Patrick's Pineapple Makeover
BUT IT'S YOUR TURN, SPONGEBOB!
EELS AND ESCALATORS CAN WAIT, PATRICK!
TRY NOT TO WRECK THE PLACE WHILE I'M GONE!
HAHAHAHA!
SLAM!
"WRECK THE PLACE!" HOW CLUMSY DOES HE THINK I--
SNAP!
GUH!
WHAM! WHAM! WHAM! WHAM! WHAM!
SPONGEBOB'S AUTOGRAPHED PICTURE OF MERMAID MAN AND BARNACLE BOY!
NO-O-O! I HIT A PIPE!
SPLOOSH!
THERE GOES SPONGEBOB'S TV...
... AND HIS GUMBALL MACHINE...
meow.
...AND GARY!
I KNEW YOU'D WRECK THE PLACE!
GOTTA CLEAN UP BEFORE SPONGEBOB GETS HOME!
NET...
...TOO...
...SMALL!

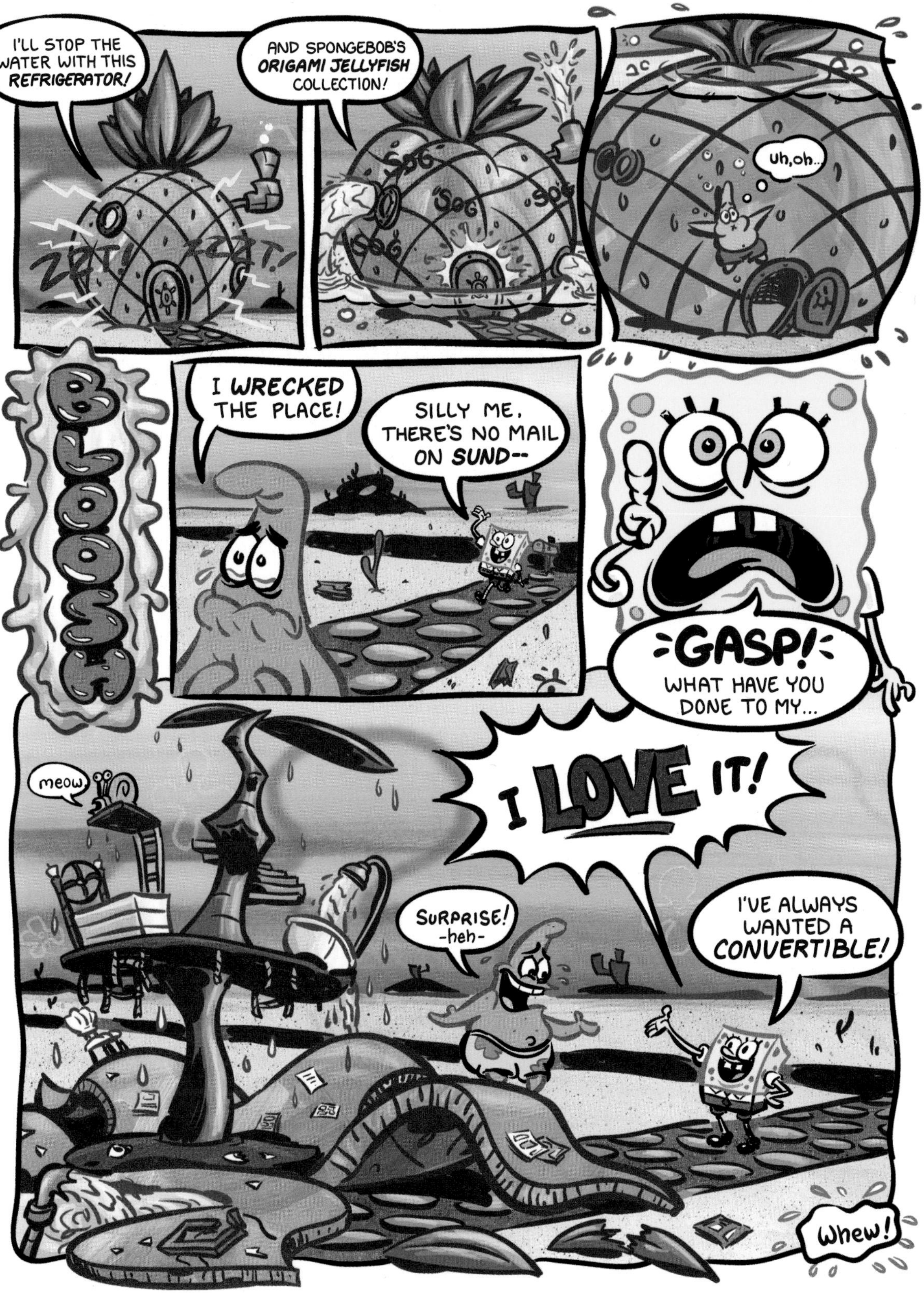
I'LL STOP THE WATER WITH THIS **REFRIGERATOR!**
AND SPONGEBOB'S ***ORIGAMI JELLYFISH*** COLLECTION!
ZZT!
ZZZT!
SOG
SOG
SOG
SOG
uh,oh...
BLOOSH
I **WRECKED** THE PLACE!
SILLY ME, THERE'S NO MAIL ON **SUND--**
GASP! WHAT HAVE YOU DONE TO MY...
I **LOVE** IT!
meow
SURPRISE! -heh-
I'VE ALWAYS WANTED A **CONVERTIBLE!**
Whew!

SANDY GOES ON A TEAR

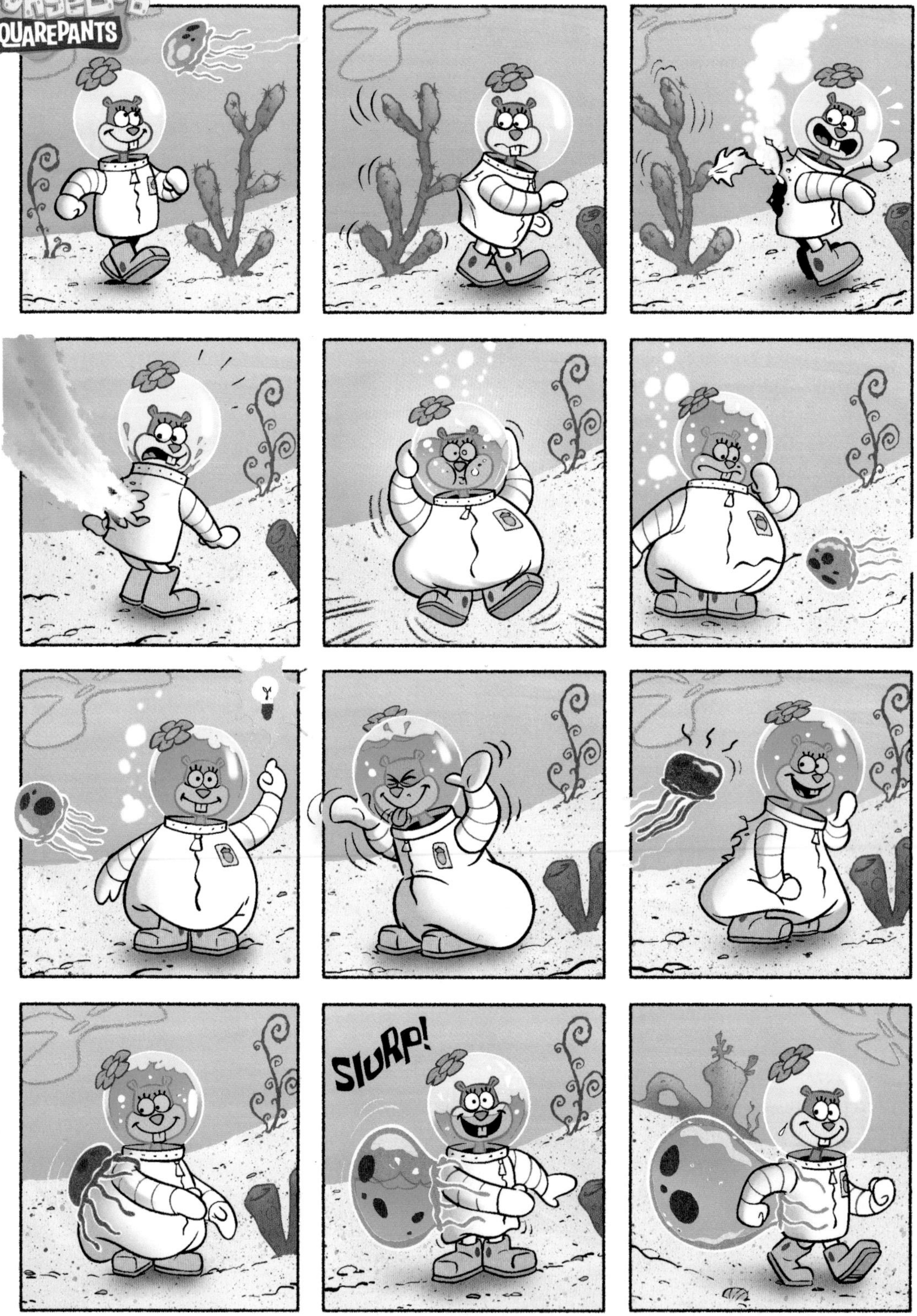
SLURP!